Excellent

P9-DET-085

WORLD OF BOOKS
8810 HILLCROFT
HOUSTON TEXAS 77096
713 721 6866

A PUBLIC KISS

"Hart."

"Yes?"

"You must let me go. Someone will see us."

"And what if they do?" he murmured softly. "Surely engaged couples are expected to indulge in an occasional kiss?"

Her eyes widened in shock. "Not in the midst of the park."

"It is somewhat public for my taste." He offered a lift of his shoulder, even as a wicked glimmer of determination smoldered to life in his eyes. "Still, beggars as they say cannot be choosers."

"Oh."

His gaze dropped to the lush temptation of her lips. Within his mind, he was calculating precisely what sort of kiss he should offer. Stark and passionate, he concluded. Something designed to send a virgin into fluttering panic. At the same moment his head was lowering to cover her mouth with his own and any sensible thought was lost in a cloud of lavender pleasure . . .

BOOKS BY DEBBIE RALEIGH

Lord Carlton's Courtship

Lord Mumford's Minx

A Bride for Lord Challmond

A Bride for Lord Wickton

A Bride for Lord Brasleigh

The Christmas Wish

The Valentine Wish

The Wedding Wish

A Proper Marriage

A Convenient Marriage

A Scandalous Marriage

My Lord Vampire

My Lord Eternity

My Lord Immortality

Miss Frazer's Adventure

The Wedding Clause

Published by Zebra Books

The Wedding Clause

Debbie Raleigh

ZEBRA BOOKS
Kensington Publishing Corp.
www.kensingtonbooks.com

ZEBRA BOOKS are published by

Kensington Publishing Corp.
850 Third Avenue
New York, NY 10022

Copyright © 2005 by Debbie Raleigh

All rights reserved. No part of this book may be reproduced in any form or by any means without the prior written consent of the Publisher, excepting brief quotes used in reviews.

If you purchased this book without a cover you should be aware that this book is stolen property. It was reported as "unsold and destroyed" to the Publisher and neither the Author nor the Publisher has received any payment for this "stripped book."

All Kensington titles, imprints, and distributed lines are available at special quantity discounts for bulk purchases for sales promotion, premiums, fund-raising, educational, or institutional use.

Special book excerpts or customized printings can also be created to fit specific needs. For details, write or phone the office of the Kensington Special Sales Manager: Attn. Special Sales Department. Kensington Publishing Corp., 850 Third Avenue, New York, NY 10022. Phone: 1-800-221-2647.

Zebra and the Z logo Reg. U.S. Pat. & TM Off.

ISBN 0-8217-7825-0

First Printing: June 2005
10 9 8 7 6 5 4 3 2 1

Printed in the United States of America

Chapter One

"What the devil! Is this some damnable jest?"

The slender, rather pale solicitor gave a nervous twitch as the angry nobleman stormed toward his desk, a wad of papers clutched in his hand.

The poor gentleman had reason to be twitchy. Anthony Elkington, Viscount Woodhart, known to his friends simply as Hart, was an intimidating force under the best of circumstances. Not only tall, he possessed the hard, relentless strength of a well-honed soldier. He had also been blessed, or perhaps cursed, with the beauty of Lucifer himself. A wide brow, thick ebony hair, features that had been chiseled by a master's hand and stunning midnight black eyes that smoldered with a relentless power all added to his aura of invincibility.

Women coveted him, even when they shivered at the hint of danger that cloaked his large form. Gentlemen flatly refused to cross his will.

At least a wise gentleman did so.

Unfortunately, Mr. Grady was in no position to be wise. Swallowing heavily, he clutched the arms of his chair as he valiantly struggled to overcome his natural instinct to bolt toward safety.

"N . . . no, sir," he managed to croak. "'Tis no jest."

"You expect me to believe that this ridiculous will is legal? Clearly my grandmother was out of her wits," Hart growled.

"I . . . yes, I mean no. That is, the will is perfectly legal, my lord, and I assure you that Lady Woodhart was in sound wits when it was drafted."

"Impossible. No one in their sound wits would think that I would ever wed Miss Conwell. Not if she were the last maiden in all of England."

"I believe your grandmother was very fond of Miss Conwell."

"Indeed." The black eyes abruptly hardened with a lethal glare. "She was also fond of that damnable parrot, Mr. Meeks. Am I expected to wed him as well?"

"I . . . no, certainly not." The words came out as a squeak. "Perhaps if you would have your own solicitor review the will, he could assure you that it is all perfectly legal and straightforward."

"No, I do not bloody wish to contact my solicitor." Hart struggled to maintain his composure. No easy task when his hands itched to wring the scrawny neck of Mr. Grady. Damn it all. It was difficult enough to have lost the grandmother he adored. A woman who had raised him after his parents had died when he was just sixteen and had been an indomitable source of strength in his life. Now to realize she had betrayed him in such a nefarious manner was nearly unbearable. No. He gave a small shake of his head. It was not his grandmother who had betrayed him. It was that damnable . . . vixen who had managed to worm her way into his grandmother's heart and, more importantly, into her fortune.

He had attempted to warn his grandmother when she first insisted that she desired Miss Conwell as her companion that the minx was nothing but trouble. Unfortunately, Lady Woodhart was quite as stubborn as himself and nothing would convince her that the young maiden was nothing more than a clever charlatan. "I want you to explain in words clear enough for my feeble brain to comprehend how you allowed a common fortune hunter to take advantage of my grandmother in such a disgraceful manner."

Well aware the looming gentleman could no doubt twist him into a knot as intricate as the one that currently graced his starched cravat, Mr. Grady carefully considered his words.

"Actually Miss Conwell was no more aware of the contents of the will than you were, my lord. And I fear just as displeased when she discovered the terms."

Hart offered a short, humorless laugh. "Oh yes, I can just imagine that she was utterly devastated to discover she had the opportunity to get her greedy hands upon near thirty thousand pounds. What fortune hunting Jezebel would not be displeased?"

Mr. Grady pinched his features to thin disapproval. "I believe you do Miss Conwell a grave injustice, my lord. She was quite devoted to Lady Woodhart and brought her much happiness in her last months."

Well bully for her, Hart thought angrily. He hoped she choked on her bloody devotion.

Then, with an effort, he forced himself to contain his raging fury. As much as he might desire to deny the truth, his grandmother had enjoyed the companionship of Miss Conwell. She had claimed the younger woman quite brightened her days with her gentle humor and sweet temperament. And whether the chit had only been angling to feather her nest with his grandmother's considerable wealth or not, she had tended to Lady Woodhart with unwavering care during her last painful months.

Still, it had been her job as a companion to tend to her employer, a voice whispered in the back of his mind. And no one, no matter how generous of nature, could possibly believe her efforts were worth thirty thousand pounds.

"Very well, if you believe that she should receive some reward for her care of Grandmother, then I am perfectly willing to offer an annuity that will allow her a measure of independence," he graciously conceded. "She could not expect more."

The pinched countenance of the solicitor did not ease, despite his perfectly reasonable offer. "A very handsome gesture, my lord, unfortunately . . ."

"Good. Then contact Miss Conwell and inform her of my decision, and I will . . ."

"Unfortunately," the solicitor continued in dogged tones, "the will is quite specific. The thirty thousand pounds will be divided equally between you and Miss Conwell on Christmas day, but only after the wedding ceremony has been performed at the family chapel. If either you or Miss Conwell fails to arrive for the wedding, then the entire fortune will go to the one who does appear. If neither of you arrive, then the money will go to the Woodhart Charity for the Disadvantaged."

Although Hart had read the damnable will on a thousand occasions over the past week, he thought his head might actually explode at once again hearing the outrageous terms.

Damn it all, his grandmother must have been daft. She knew better than anyone that he and Molly Conwell could not bear the sight of each other. Gads, they had only to be in the same room for the both of them to be bristling and snarling like angry hounds.

She thought him a heartless rake. He thought her a callow fortune hunter.

To even consider the notion of taking her as his wife . . .

Hellfire. It was enough to cause any sane gentleman to break out in a rash.

"This is ludicrous. My grandmother could be stubborn but not even she could possibly desire me to wed a woman I would most certainly strangle within moments of the ceremony," he muttered. "There has to be some means of proving she was not in her proper wits when the will was written."

Mr. Grady licked his thin lips. "She did possess the foresight to have myself as well as her doctor and her steward present when the will was made. It would be near impossible to prove she was too feebleminded to decide how she desired her wealth to be distributed. And certainly not before Christmas day."

The solicitor was right, blast his scrawny hide. It was already the middle of November. He had less than six weeks to find some means of outwitting the ridiculous will.

Or doing away with Miss Conwell.

Perhaps the preferable choice.

"Well, this is a bloody mess."

"Yes, well, it will no doubt work out in the end," the solicitor murmured in weak tones. "In my experience, arranged marriages are quite often for the best. Far less awkward and messy than supposed love matches."

The vein in his temple throbbed even harder. "Indeed? And what of blatant blackmail? Are you in favor of that as well?"

There was no mistaking the furious edge that threaded through his voice. The gaunt gentleman abruptly scooted his chair back a few inches as if ridiculously presuming he could flee before Hart could manage to shake him senseless.

"Please recall, my lord, that this . . . desire for you to wed Miss Conwell was solely the wish of Lady Woodhart," he at last muttered cowardly. "I am merely acting as a messenger."

Hart checked his scathing retort. Perhaps he was being a tad unreasonable. Although the solicitor could be branded an incompetent twit, he had not actually been to blame for his grandmother's mad flight of fancy.

No. The blame could be laid squarely upon the shoulders of Miss Molly Conwell.

"Bloody hell." His nose flared with distaste. "It

appears I have no choice but to meet with Miss Conwell and convince her to put an end to this madness."

A hint of relief rippled over Mr. Grady's narrow countenance. Clearly, he vastly preferred to turn Hart over to Miss Conwell. No doubt a wise decision, Hart acknowledged wryly. In his current temper he could only be pressed so far.

"Yes, I believe that would be the best solution."

"Fine." Hart leaned upon the desk to glare directly in the pasty white face. "I hope for all our sakes that she is willing to be reasonable. No one, including you, Mr. Grady, will enjoy the outcome if she is not."

With his parting shot successfully delivered, Hart turned on his heel and swept from the carpeted office, his heavily caped greatcoat billowing behind his rigid form.

The cottage perched upon the isolated bluff not far south of London was held together by little more than a handful of nails and a prayer. Without the stones were crumbled and the thatching in dire need of repair; within the cramped rooms were damp and possessed the ever-present scent of must. A hovel that was unfit for the lowest tenant, let alone Lord Canfield. Thankfully, however, it was a perfect setting for a renowned smuggler avoiding the authorities.

Pacing through the tiny parlor Andrew Conwell jammed an impatient hand through his overly long golden curls. He was young to be the current Baron, barely four and twenty years of age, and blessed with a handsome beauty that had made him an undoubted favorite of society. He also possessed the sort of charm that had caused women to flutter in delight since leaving the cradle.

Such abundance of wealth and prominence had been bound to turn any young gentleman's head. And unfortunately, Andrew had been easily tempted by the numerous hazards that London had to offer. After his parents' death nearly two years before, he had indulged in months of decadent excess. With the self-centered indulgence of sheer youth, he had gloried in his heedless entertainments, never hesitating to approach the numerous moneylenders who were anxious to offer the endless supply of wealth that a young rakehell was ever in need of.

Life was meant to be enjoyed to the fullest, he had adamantly maintained.

Until the debts had come due.

It was in that moment that Andrew had at last realized that he was more than just ruined. The moneylenders that had once seemed so benign and helpful were now threatening his very life. And worse, they had threatened his beloved sister with their vile brutality.

There had been nothing to do but make a hasty disappearance. And swiftly.

With a cleverness born of desperation, he had traveled to Europe, leaving just enough of a trail to convince his creditors that he was well out of reach before secretly slipping back across the channel to take up his current profession of smuggler.

No one knew of his whereabouts beyond Molly. To all Lord Canfield was currently continuing his life of dissipation in Italy, while those nearer the coast simply knew him as Shade, a smuggler extraordinaire.

But while he guarded his secret with his very life, his sister's brief missive had prompted him to risk all and contact her with a demand that she travel to the cottage.

Now he glared at her slender form perched delicately upon the battered chair, appearing as innocent as an angel with her glorious golden curls and flashing dimples. It was only when one happened to glance at the dark brown eyes that held more than a hint of stubborn intelligence that the vision of sweet compliance was firmly shattered.

"No, Molly," he said as he reached the empty grate and turned to send her a warning glare. "I absolutely forbid you to have anything to do with the man. They do not call him the Heartless Viscount for nothing."

Well prepared for the inevitable lecture, Molly Conwell merely folded her hands in her lap. In truth, she had considered ignoring her brother's curt letter. She had known he would attempt to undermine her decision. A waste of both of their time. But the fear that he might do something absurdly risky, such as appearing in London himself, had forced her to enter the carriage he had sent for her and travel to the remote cottage.

"Fah." She gave a faint sniff. "I am not frightened of Lord Woodhart, Andrew."

Her brother planted his hands upon his hips, his blue eyes flashing with annoyance. "Then you are a fool. For God's sake, he is one of the most powerful and wealthy men in all of England. That is not even to mention the fact that he is a ruthless enough demon to eat young maidens like you for breakfast. To even consider crossing his will is madness."

Molly swallowed a sigh. Gads, she was not utterly stupid. She knew quite well that Hart was a dangerous opponent. Had she not endured his sharp dislike and blatant insults for the past year? And now with his worst fears of her being a fortune hunter seemingly confirmed, he was bound to be even more difficult.

That, however, did not sway her determination. For the first time in over a year there appeared to be the faintest hope that her brother could somehow put an end to his debts and return to his rightful place at Oakgrove. Even more importantly, he could put an end to his perilous life as a smuggler.

She would endure any torture for such a gift.

"You would have me simply toss away the solution to all our troubles?" she demanded softly. "That is madness, Andrew."

He gave a slow shake of his head, his handsome features set in somber lines. "Not *our* troubles, Molly. My troubles. It was my selfish stupidity that led to our current difficulties and I will be the one to solve them."

"How?"

He stiffened at her abrupt demand. "Allow me to worry about that."

"I will not. You are being absurd."

An unmistakable flare of pain rippled over his countenance. It was a pain that tugged at Molly's heart. Whatever his mistakes in the past, she did not doubt that her brother suffered from regret and self-reproach every moment of every day.

"I am being absurd because I will not allow my sister to sell herself to save my own hide?" he retorted with an edge of bitterness in his voice.

She slowly rose to her feet to cross the uneven floor and place a hand upon his rigid arm. "I have told you, Andrew, I do not intend to wed Lord Woodhart. All I need do is arrive at the chapel on Christmas day and I will have thirty thousand pounds. Enough to pay off your creditors and even to begin repairs upon Oakgrove."

Andrew offered a short, disbelieving laugh at her confident words. "Just arrive at the chapel? You believe that Lord Woodhart will allow you to blithely snatch a fortune from beneath his very nose? I never thought you such a goose wit."

She gave a faint shrug. "To prevent me from acquiring the fortune he must also arrive at the chapel and risk having me as his wife. A fate you must know he considers worse than death."

"That all depends upon whose death you refer to, Molly."

Her eyes widened at his grim tone. "Good heavens, do you mean to imply that you fear Lord Woodhart might murder me for the paltry sum of thirty thousand pounds?"

Astonishingly, her teasing words merely deepened

Andrew's fierce scowl. "It is not a paltry sum, as you well know."

"Not for us, but Lord Woodhart is hardly in need of additional wealth," she pointed out with a careful logic.

"A nobleman is always in need of wealth, Molly." He grimaced with self-derision. "It is extraordinarily expensive to be a gentleman of leisure, as I learned to my regret. Besides, whatever his need or lack of need for a fortune, it will be his pride that will demand he not allow a fortune hunter to steal what he believes to rightfully belong to him."

Molly abruptly stepped back, a frown marring her wide brow. "Andrew, that is a horrid thing to say. I am no fortune hunter."

He held up a soothing hand. "Of course, you are not. But Lord Woodhart has made it obvious that he suspects you of nefarious purposes since you first took a position with his grandmother."

Well, she could hardly argue with that. His high and mighty lordship had made her life with Lady Woodhart a near misery with his unrelenting suspicion. Of course, she had begun to presume that he made a sport of causing everyone misery. For all his astonishing male beauty and undoubted success among the fairer sex, he seemed to take perverse pleasure in strolling through society like a predator on the prowl for his next meal.

"The man would suspect a saint of nefarious purposes," she retorted dryly. "No doubt his heart is so black he cannot conceive that there are those who can genuinely care for one another."

"Precisely." Andrew regarded her with a steady gaze. "Which is why you will have nothing to do with the scoundrel."

"But . . ."

"No, Molly. Lady Woodhart was clearly out of her wits to even contemplate allowing you to be at the mercy of such a notorious rogue. I, however, possess fully functioning faculties and I will not allow you to place yourself in such danger."

Less than a year younger than her sibling, Molly was not at all accustomed to obeying his stern commands. Especially when he was not making the least amount of sense.

Planting her hands upon her hips, she met him glare for glare.

"You are a fine one to talk, Andrew. You court danger every night of your life."

He at least possessed the grace to redden at her reprimand. "It is not so bad as that."

"Yes, it is. I hate knowing that you are forever taking risks that could have you transported or worse. That is not even to mention the danger of those horrid men from London discovering you have returned to England." She gave a shake of her head. "You should be at Oakgrove tending to your crops and raising your children, not hiding in this damp cottage like a skulking criminal."

Without warning, Andrew turned on his heel and rigidly paced to gaze out the window. For a long moment a heavy silence filled the oppressive air, and then with a deep sigh he turned to regard her with shadowed eyes.

"Molly, you should leave before it grows dark.

This is no place for a lady. Especially not one who is beautiful enough to tempt my crew to mutiny."

If she had hoped that her fervent words would convince him to agree to her daring plan, she was doomed to disappointment. For all his youth her brother possessed a full share of Conwell pride.

Clearly, she would have to keep her schemes to herself.

"Very well," she murmured.

"Will you go to Cousin May?"

She suppressed a shudder at the mere thought. Her elderly cousin lived as a near recluse in the wilds of Devonshire with a habit of treating her visitors as unpaid servants there to pander her every whim.

"Actually I believe I shall return to London." She paused, knowing that her brother was bound to offer up yet more protests at her choice of destinations. "Georgie has invited me to stay with her."

As if on cue, the finely chiseled features hardened with distaste. "Georgie? Gads, Molly, I realize you consider her a friend, but the woman is not at all a suitable companion."

Her own countenance firmed into an expression of stubborn annoyance. Really, the prickly dislike between Georgie and Andrew was becoming absurd beyond bearing. Georgiana, Lady Falker, had been her closest friend since they had been in the nursery. And most aggravatingly, when they were young, Andrew had been just as devoted to the charming maiden. What occurred to turn them into fierce enemies, Molly had never discovered, but whatever had happened Georgie had abruptly wed a man twice her age who had died within weeks of their marriage, and Andrew had taken off for London where he had managed to efficiently destroy his future.

Neither would admit what precisely had set them at odds, but neither of them could be within the same room without coming to near blows.

"Andrew," she chided with a frown.

"You cannot deny the truth, Molly," he growled. "She is the biggest flirt in London and is rarely more than a breath away from scandal."

"She is also my dearest friend and I will not have a word said against her. Besides, I shall only be staying with her until I can find a new position."

His anger abruptly drained away to leave him appearing heartbreakingly harassed. "Blast. I am sorry, Molly."

She gave a small sniff. "Well, you should be. Georgie is . . ."

"Oh, not that." His hands lifted to wearily scrub his face. "I am sorry I have been such a bloody worthless brother. It is because of me that you are forced to hire yourself out as a lowly servant rather than possessing the life you were born to enjoy. You should be lady of the manor at Oakgrove, or dancing your way through London ballrooms. I should be shot for what I have done to you."

Her heart twisted with sympathy at the dark reproach that laced his voice. She moved to grasp his hand in a tight grip.

"Please do not say such things, Andrew."

"Why should I not? I am utterly to blame." He gave a disgusted shake of his head. "And the truth of the matter is that I cannot promise the future will be any better."

Molly briefly allowed herself to lean against his strength. It felt astonishingly comforting. It had been so very long since she had been able to depend upon anyone but herself.

"It will be," she whispered softly.

"My sweet Molly." Andrew dropped a kiss upon her curls before firmly stepping back. "Promise me you will take care of yourself and not allow Georgie to lure you into trouble."

She smiled ruefully. "I promise."

Reaching beneath his rather shabby coat, he pulled out a small leather bag and pressed it into her hand. "Here."

"What is it?"

"A few quid." He gave a shrug of his broad shoulder. "You shall need it until you can find a new position."

She gave a firm shake of her head, knowing that her brother would no doubt take unnerving risks to regain the small fortune.

"No, Andrew, I still possess the very generous salary that Lady Woodhart paid me. I have no need for this."

He crossed his arms against his chest, his chin jutting out in an ominous manner. "Then buy yourself something pretty while you are in London. It is the least I can do for my sister."

Molly wavered. As much as she disliked the notion of Andrew placing himself in danger, she could not blatantly wound his pride by refusing his gift. He felt guilty enough that he could not provide what he believed she deserved.

With a small nod of her head, she placed the bag in her reticule, intending to place the money in the first offering box she passed. She would not accept ill-gotten wealth, even to please her brother. Reluctantly she moved to collect the heavy cape she had left beside the door. Once prepared to battle the chilled November air, she turned back to send Andrew a concerned glance.

"Be careful, Andrew. I could not bear for any-thing to happen to you."

He smiled wryly. "The devil takes care of his own, my dear. Now be off with you."

"Good-bye."

She had pulled open the door when her brother abruptly took a step forward. "Molly."

With a lift of her brows, she paused upon the threshold. "Yes?"

"Stay away from Lord Woodhart," he warned in fierce tones.

Unable to utter a blatant lie, Molly merely smiled sweetly as she gave a small curtsey. "Do not fret, Andrew. All will be well."

Chapter Two

Despite being quite late when Molly at last returned to London, she directed the driver to the elegant Mayfair Square where she had resided with Lady Woodhart. There was no use in putting off the inevitable, she told herself. She had to accept that her beloved employer was gone, and that she must once again confront an uncertain future.

Requesting that the driver await her return, Molly retrieved her key to the door and let herself into the silent house. There was little use in disturbing the servants. And in truth, she was not inclined to endure the inevitable tearful parting with those she had grown so close to. Later she would return and say her good-byes, she promised as she slipped through the shadowed foyer and toward the curved staircase. She would even bring with her a few trifling gifts to show her appreciation for their efforts in making her feel comfortable in the household.

In the meantime, she would gather her few belongings and remove them to Georgie's townhouse.

Weary from her exhausting day, Molly climbed

to the upper floor that housed her former chambers and moved down the wide hall. She had nearly reached the door to her rooms when a large form detached itself from the wall to abruptly block her path.

Her breath vanished as she pressed a hand to her racing heart.

"Oh."

The apparition stepped closer, allowing a slanting shaft of moonlight to bathe over the silken raven curls and starkly masculine countenance. No, not a demon, as she had first feared, but as close to one as it made no difference.

As if sensing her dark thoughts a sardonic smile curved Lord Woodhart's full lips.

"So, the prodigal fiancée at last returns," he murmured in those tones that always reminded her of black silk.

Molly determinedly gathered her courage about her. This man possessed the ability to unnerve the staunchest of souls. And usually with nothing more than an imperious lift of his brow.

Well, she would not be intimidated, she silently swore. Nor would she be bullied. Andrew's future depended upon her. She would not fail.

"My lord." She forced herself to meet the glittering black eyes, ignoring the odd prickles that raced over her skin. "You frightened me."

That famous brow slowly arched as he blatantly allowed his gaze to sweep over her small form in a dismissive manner.

"Surely you did not believe I would leave my grandmother's home unattended? Who knows what sort of devious, untrustworthy creature of the night might crawl off the street?"

Her hands curled at her side. Oh, the pleasure of smacking that smug expression from his face. Unfortunately, she had been raised a lady and as such was forced to squash her rather violent desires.

Instead she forced a smile to her stiff lips.

"I must admit that devious, untrustworthy creatures were not a danger that I had considered until this moment." She pointedly allowed her own gaze to sweep his large, decidedly male form.

"While I, Miss Conwell, have considered one in particular any time these past twelve months."

Oh yes, just one punch. Directly to that arrogant nose.

"How tedious it must be for you to forever harbor suspicion of all you meet."

"It is far more tedious to forever have my suspicions confirmed," he drawled softly.

Molly stiffened in embarrassment. Ridiculous, of course. She had not desired Lady Woodhart's wealth. And certainly not at the risk of being irretrievably stuck with this aggravating gentleman. It was Lady Woodhart who had insisted upon that absurd will. She had done nothing but be a friend and companion to the elderly woman.

Of course, she could not deny that she fully intended to take advantage of her unexpected windfall, she wryly acknowledged. She was not utterly selfless.

"Well then, I shall leave you to your vigilant guard, my lord," she said with a mocking curtsey. "I am merely here to collect my belongings."

Intent upon sweeping past him with her nose firmly in the air, she was annoyingly halted when he smoothly shifted to stand in her path.

"You are moving your belongings?" he demanded with a narrowed gaze.

She glared into the fiercely handsome countenance. "Of course. My services are clearly no longer needed with . . . with Lady Woodhart gone."

Despite her best efforts, she could not prevent a small quiver from entering her voice as she was struck with a sharp pang of loss. Predictably, however, her display of sentiment was met with nothing more than aloof disbelief.

"Please do not bother with false tears on my account, Miss Conwell. I fear unlike my grandmother I am immune to such feminine wiles."

"Will you please remove yourself from my path?" she gritted.

"No."

"You mean to deny me my belongings?"

Even in the silvery shadows, she could sense his brooding menace. He clearly had not expected her to so readily abandon her luxurious chambers and life of ease. And he was not a man who liked being caught off guard.

"I mean for us to have a long overdue discussion of our supposed engagement, Miss Conwell," he stated in tones that defied argument. "A discussion that would have taken place this morning if you had not so mysteriously fled London."

A faint shiver of fear raced down her spine. She had never considered the notion that anyone beyond the servants might have noted her absence.

Now her stomach clenched at the mere thought of this man devoting the entire day to pondering her odd disappearance. Whatever her dislike of him, she was never foolish enough to underestimate his shrewd intelligence. If he truly put his mind to the matter, he would no doubt ferret out her brother with frightening ease.

And then . . . dear God, he would ruthlessly destroy the both of them.

"I did not flee London, my lord," she retorted in an icy tone, grimly forcing herself to meet the black gaze.

"No? Then where have you been?"

"That is none of your concern."

His eyes narrowed. "On the contrary, Miss Conwell, it is very much my concern."

Realizing that he was not about to be put off she swallowed heavily.

"I . . . I traveled to visit my old nurse who has been ill," she grudgingly forced the lie past her stiff lips.

Thankfully, his mouth curled in a mocking smile and the prickling sense of danger slowly eased.

"Another vulnerable old woman who believes your appearance of an angel is more than skin deep? Or perhaps the two of you were merely celebrating the fortune you managed to bilk?"

"Enough." Molly tugged the heavy cape closer to her chilled body. "If you would be so good as to have my belongings sent to . . ."

"Oh no. I have said that I wish to speak with you."

"Well, that is rather unfortunate since I would

as soon be boiled in tar as to spend another moment in your presence."

His lips twitched at her stilted words, his large form gliding close enough for her to catch the scent of warm male cologne.

"A tempting notion; however, you are not worth a hangman's noose. Now, Molly, do we do this as reasonable adults or do I need to toss you over my shoulder and carry you kicking and screaming to the parlor?"

She longed to defy him. She was cold, weary and not at all inclined to endure any more of his tangible contempt. Unfortunately, she did not doubt for a moment that he would forcibly haul her to the parlor. And no doubt take great pleasure in doing so.

"You are no gentleman," she informed him, even as she reluctantly allowed him to take her arm and steer her back toward the stairs.

"A fortunate thing since you are certainly no lady," he smoothly shot back.

She clamped her lips together, determined to ignore his annoying presence as they traveled through the shadowed house. A ridiculous notion, of course. She could as soon as ignore a stalking panther chained to her side.

Especially when his clinging touch was creating the most peculiar shivers along the length of her arm.

Reaching the landing, Hart turned her toward the nearby parlor. They had nearly reached the open door when the elderly butler made a sudden entrance from a side staircase.

"Good evening, sir," he murmured with a low

bow, seemingly not at all surprised to discover the nobleman in the house at such a late hour. "May I serve you tea?"

"Thank you, no. I believe we shall have need of something rather more bracing."

"Very good."

"Oh, Clark," Hart halted the dignified servant's retreat. "Please ensure we are not interrupted. I would not desire an innocent bystander to stumble into the fray."

Clark shot an alarmed glance toward the silent Molly, but at her faint nod he conceded to the inevitable. Molly inwardly shrugged. There was no use in involving the poor servants in the brewing confrontation.

"Er . . . yes, my lord."

With an insistent tug, Hart maneuvered Molly into the pale blue and ivory parlor and firmly shut the door. Only then did he at last release her to stroll casually toward the oak sideboard and plucked a crystal decanter from the tray.

"Brandy?"

She gave a vague shrug. "Why not?"

"Indeed." Pouring two glasses he turned to trace his way back to her rigid form. "Here you are."

"Thank you." Molly accepted the brandy, unnervingly aware of his piercing gaze as she took a small sip.

"I suppose you think you have been very clever, my dear?"

She took a moment to stiffen her courage before lifting her head and slipping into the dangerous role she had cast for herself.

"Clever? Yes, I believe that I have always been reasonably clever."

In the flickering candlelight, his warrior beauty was enticingly potent. Even with his rigid expression of disdain.

"I am sure you have. Women such as you usually possess some cunning. For once, however, I fear you have met your match, my sweet Molly."

"You are referring to yourself, no doubt?"

"Precisely." Lifting his glass in a small toast, he downed the amber brandy in one swallow. "And I can assure you that whatever your ability to deceive my grandmother, you have never deceived me for a moment. I had your measure from the moment you enticed your way into this household."

"Bully for you, my lord," she muttered.

His lips curled in a humorless smile. "Which is the reason when I learned of my grandmother's outrageous will my first inclination was to simply throttle you and be done with it."

Her gaze did not waver. Whatever his endless list of faults, Molly knew that he would never physically harm a woman. No matter what the provocation.

"Well, you are nothing if not predictable, my lord. I believe you have threatened to throttle me upon any number of occasions over the past months."

The arrogant nose flared at her deliberate taunt. "However, with the opportunity to contemplate the distasteful situation, much against my better judgment, I have decided to be generous."

"Then I am not to be throttled? You cannot know the depths of my relief."

Just for a moment his hands curled as if he would indeed throttle her, and then with a coiled control he set aside his glass and regarded her with cold, glittering eyes.

"I am willing to offer you one thousand pounds in return for you leaving London and promising never to trouble my family again."

The offer, as well as the undoubted threat in his tone was precisely what Molly had been expecting and she was able to conjure a faint smile as she nonchalantly strolled toward the ivory marble chimneypiece.

"A thousand pounds?"

"Far more than you deserve, but for the sake of my grandmother who possessed a rather ghastly fondness for you, I am willing to make the sacrifice."

"I see."

There was a short, tense silence during which she could feel his gaze boring into her back. "Well?" he at last gritted.

Slowly turning, she gave a lift of her brows. "I beg your pardon?"

"What is your answer?"

"Oh, forgive me. I did not believe that you truly expected a response to such an absurd offer."

His jaw knotted as he sought to contain his fury. Molly unwittingly stepped back, feeling as if the very air was pulsing with danger.

"You are a fool if you think to cross me, Molly," he rasped.

She swallowed heavily. "No, I would be a fool to accept a thousand pounds when I shall soon possess thirty thousand."

"Never."

"The only means to halt me, my lord, is to wed me." She gave a tilt of her chin. "And we both know that is as likely as Napoleon being crowned King of England."

His nose flared as he slowly, relentlessly prowled toward her. Despite her best intentions, Molly discovered herself abruptly backing until she was flatly pressed against the satin wall paneling. Even then he did not halt but continued until his hard form was nearly touching her own, his hands braced against the wall on either side of her head.

"If you think to force my price up, my love, you are playing a dangerous game. My offer is more than fair."

Molly bit the inside of her lip as he loomed above her. Good heavens, she had never had a gentleman stand so close. At least no gentleman beyond Andrew. She should no doubt be terrified, but instead she discovered herself shivering as the oddest tingles raced through her blood.

"No, it is an insult," she forced herself to mutter. "Now, if that is all . . ."

"I was mistaken, Miss Conwell."

Her heart skittered as his warm breath brushed her cheeks. "I beg your pardon?"

"I said you were clever. It is obvious you are no more than a fool."

Well, Molly could hardly argue with his logic. Certainly, no one but a complete fool would defy this large, decidedly furious male who could no doubt break her in two without a blink of the eye. But for all her stupidity, she could not smother the thought of Andrew in that horrid cottage, in ever present danger of being caught or killed.

She would face Lucifer himself to rescue her brother.

"I suppose we shall discover, my lord." Gathering her nerve, Molly abruptly ducked beneath his arm and swiftly charged toward the nearby door before she could be halted. She had endured quite enough for one evening. "For now you must excuse me. I must have my rest if I am to begin shopping for my trousseau."

She heard him growl her name as she rushed out of the room and down the hall. Thankfully, however, he did not follow and she was allowed to reach the front door relatively unscathed. Still, it was not until she was in the awaiting carriage and traveling toward Georgie's townhouse that she at last heaved a sigh of relief.

Oh, sweet heavens. She was in the fire now.

"You understand what I require of you?" Hart demanded, offering the young maid the sort of quelling frown that made the stiffest of resolves falter.

"I . . ." The awkwardly plain maiden with frizzy brown curls and protruding front teeth shifted uneasily. When Hart had first approached her in the marketplace, she had been giddily pleased to have caught the notice of such an elegant, heart-achingly handsome gentleman. Surely only in her most treasured fantasies was such a wondrous event possible? Now, she desperately wished that he had blithely ignored her, as every other gentleman was wont to do. "I suppose I do, sir."

Only with an effort did Hart manage to smother his burst of impatience. After nearly a week of brooding and scheming to put an end to his unwelcome engagement, he would be a fool to ruin all now. It was imperative that he win the cooperation of this maid if he were to succeed.

"Is something troubling you?" he asked in what he hoped were soothing tones.

The servant grimaced as she shifted the heavy basket of bread to her other arm. "Well, it ain't hardly proper to be spying upon my lady's guest."

"Spying? Nonsense. I merely request that you keep me informed of my fiancée's various plans. She is not at all accustomed to London society and I wish to ensure that she does not make any unfortunate errors that might bring her embarrassment." He summoned his most potent smile. "Besides which, if I am perfectly honest, I will admit that I am besotted enough to regret being away from her for even a moment. At least with your assistance I shall be able to adjust my own schedule so that I may be with her whenever possible."

The hapless maid blinked beneath the power of his lazy, utterly seductive smile. "Oh."

Hart gave a lift of his slender hand. "You no doubt consider me a romantic fool?"

"Aye, most romantic," she sighed.

"Then you agree to be my partner?"

She bit her lip in confusion. "What of Lady Falker? If she were to discover what I am about she would likely have me thrown out of the house. I cannot afford to lose me position."

"Do not fear," he murmured softly. "No one shall ever know."

"But . . ."

"Besides which, I intend to handsomely reward you for whatever information you might have to offer. More than enough to compensate for any risk you might be taking."

An unmistakable glitter of greed entered the pale blue eyes, and Hart silently congratulated his devious valet who had been the one to select this maid as his most likely ally in the Falker household.

"I suppose it would do no harm," she slowly convinced herself.

"Certainly not. In truth, you shall be of great assistance to Miss Conwell, even if she is not to know that you are her secret guardian angel."

"Me a guardian angel?" The maid gave a shrill giggle. "Lor', what would me ma say?"

Hart sternly kept his smile in place. "Do not forget that this . . . agreement is between the two of us. No one else must know."

"Oh, aye, I shall not be forgetting."

Knowing that he could not linger without attracting unwelcome notice, Hart offered a faint bow of his head. "Good. My valet will contact you each morning to discover what you have learned. He will also bring your reward. Is that satisfactory?"

She gave a faint pout. "I shan't be seeing you?"

"No doubt we shall encounter each other upon

occasion," he murmured vaguely. "Now I must be on my way. Do not fail me."

"I won't," the maid promised, heaving a soulful sigh as Hart abruptly turned upon his heel and melted into the rather ragged crowd.

Walking with confident strides and a steely expression that intimidated even the most desperate of pickpockets, Hart made his way through the maze of cluttered streets toward the more fashionable neighborhoods. Although the chilled November breeze tugged at his greatcoat and threatened to send his high beaver hat tumbling from his head, he felt considerably more in charity with the world than he had since his disturbing confrontation with Miss Conwell at his grandmother's home.

The minx thought she could steal a fortune from beneath his very nose? A fortune that rightfully belonged to him? Well, she would soon enough discover that no one bested the Viscount Woodhart. And certainly not a cold-hearted vixen who would blatantly take advantage of a confused old woman.

Unfortunately, bribery had not swayed her. Nor did it seem she could be bullied into conceding defeat. Blast her annoying arrogance. It had taken several brandy sodden days to at last hit upon his current solution.

Women were unpredictable, cunning creatures. But he was well aware that they all possessed one weakness. One certain weakness.

Vanity.

Miss Conwell might not be bribed or bullied, but with the proper amount of public humiliation she would be happy enough to accept his generous offer and disappear from society. It was as inevitable as the sun rising in the morning.

The faintest smile touched his lips as he continued onward and at last turned the corner onto Bond Street. Then, as his gaze lazily drifted over the handful of ladies and maids that swayed along the pavement, he jerked to a sudden halt. Bloody hell. Miss Molly Conwell. Standing before an elegant millinery as bold as brass.

Narrowing his gaze, he studied the delicate form attired in a sturdy blue gown and the rather plain chip bonnet. She should have easily been overlooked as a dowd with her pale coloring and lack of sophistication. But as always, whenever she was near, Hart discovered his gaze lingering upon the purity of her elegant profile, the determined jut of her chin and golden curls that lay like the softest satin against her porcelain skin.

It was not that the minx fascinated him; he was always swift to reassure himself. He did not shadow her movements and covertly stare at her because her features held a sweet innocence that was a balm to a gentleman jaded by far too much experience. Or because the startling dark eyes held an intelligence that was all too rare.

It was quite simply the irony that a maiden who possessed the appearance of an angel could harbor a heart as black as the netherworld that attracted his attention.

And the knowledge that only a fool would turn his back on the deceitful chit. Not unless he desired a knife stuck in it.

Yes, that was most certainly the answer, he

sternly told himself, willing the odd tautness of his chest to ease and determinedly stroked his justifiable anger to full flame.

She might look like an angel on the surface, but within she was a ruthless jade who would steal his inheritance if he faltered for even a moment.

With a deep breath, he squared his shoulders. Although his schemes had not taken into account bumping into Miss Conwell in the midst of Bond Street, there was no reason he could not use it fully to his advantage.

The sooner he began his campaign of humiliation the sooner she would be fleeing back beneath whatever rock she had crawled from, he told himself sternly.

Assuming the bored nonchalance of a true gentleman of style, Hart strolled forward, making a point to tip his hat at the various females and shopkeepers who openly gawked at his large male form. For once he did not abhor the swarm of excitement his presence always managed to stir. The more attention he could gather, the better.

As if sensing the sudden flutter of excitement behind her, Molly slowly turned to regard Hart's relentless approach. Even at a distance he could detect her eyes widening in alarm and her slender form stiffening. He allowed his lips to curve into a small smile. It was obvious that she was preparing herself for yet another battle.

Well, she was about to endure one, although it would not be the sort she was anticipating.

Hart slowed his steps as he neared his unwanted fiancée, deliberately snaring her uncertain gaze. Ever closer he approached, keeping her gaze locked with his own until at last she was forced to sweep a reluctant curtsey.

It was the moment he had been awaiting and even as she straightened Hart arrogantly turned his head and with firm steps swept past her without the least hint of acknowledgment.

He heard her gasp of outrage at his deliberate cut, but oddly it was the sweet scent of lavender that seemed to cling to the air that he noted. Dash it all. He had always possessed a weakness for lavender. Especially when it was warmed by soft porcelain skin . . .

No. Keeping his feet moving forward he sternly chastised his ridiculous flare of awareness. What did he care if the woman drenched herself in lavender from morning till night? Or that those soft brown eyes had darkened with something that might have been pain? All that mattered was that he had delivered his first blow.

By this evening every drawing room in London would be filled with the tantalizing gossip that Lord Woodhart had given Miss Conwell, a woman quietly whispered to be his own fiancée, the cut direct. She would be the source of undoubted speculation and amusement for days.

Precisely what he desired.

Oh yes, a most satisfactory beginning, he told himself, urging a smile to his stiff lips.

Chapter Three

It was several hours later when Hart arrived at his club for a quiet dinner. When he had first prepared for the evening, he had considered making his way through the various London soirees and assemblies. It would be the perfect opportunity to discover if his insult earlier in the day was making the usual rounds.

But even as he called for his carriage, he had grimaced at the thought of enduring hours of banal chatter and the relentless pursuit of the more predatory females. Gads, what a sorry waste of an evening. And for what? The gossip would spread whether or not he made an appearance. Perhaps even more swiftly if his presence were not there to stifle any stray rumors.

His decision made, he had commanded his driver to the discreet club where he avoided the more boisterous gaming rooms and instead settled himself in a shadowed corner. He had just finished an excellent beefsteak and was about to enjoy a fine cognac when his privacy was abruptly invaded.

"Ah, Hart," Lord Thorpe drawled as he audaciously deposited his lean form in a nearby seat and stretched out his long legs. "What a delightful surprise."

Hart regarded the eldest son of the Duke of Harmond with a wry expression. In truth, it was rather like looking in a mirror. As maternal cousins they both shared the same raven hair, dark eyes and powerful features of their distant ancestors. They also shared more than a fair measure of the same pride and arrogance. Which no doubt explained why they had devoted their early years to being fierce competitors. It did not matter if it were sports, cards, horses or women; they battled for supremacy in all.

Thankfully, maturity had managed to mellow their relationship to one of easy friendship, as well as deepening the bonds of loyalty. Thorpe was perhaps the only person left in the world that Hart truly trusted.

Lifting a hand toward the uniformed servant, Hart waited until his cousin was served with a glass of cognac before responding.

"I would hardly think my presence is much of a surprise, delightful or otherwise," he drawled. "I do spend any number of evenings here."

The dark eyes, so similar to his own, glittered with wicked amusement. "Ah, but that was before you managed to acquire a fiancée, dear cousin. Surely now you are expected to attend those tedious society events so that you might trail behind your intended like a devoted hound and snarl when another gentleman might stray too close?"

Hart stiffened. Although he knew that there had already been whispers of his grandmother's absurd will, Thorpe was the first to actually confront him with rumors.

"Presuming that I did possess a fiancée, I can assure you the last place I would ever be is trailing behind her at tedious society events, or anywhere else for that matter."

A raven brow arched at his edged words. "Presuming? Do you not know if you possess a fiancée or not?"

His lips thinned in annoyance. "If you have heard the rumors, then you know quite well that my grandmother's inheritance hinges upon my wedding Miss Conwell."

"Then you do possess a fiancée." Thorpe leaned his head against the leather of his wing chair, a speculative expression upon his lean countenance. "I must say I am rather hurt. How much effort could it take to scribble me a missive of your impending nuptials?" He abruptly widened his eyes. "Good God, I am invited to the wedding am I not?"

"Do not be more of an ass than you need be, Thorpe. There is not going to be any wedding," Hart snapped.

"Then you have decided to relinquish your inheritance? A rather generous stroke of fortune for Miss Conwell. And a decidedly uncharacteristic display of nobility for you, Hart."

Hart rolled his eyes heavenward. No one could be more irritating than Thorpe when he put his mind to it.

"No, I do not intend to relinquish my fortune. Certainly not to Miss Conwell. I will see every handed over to the bloody Woodhart Charity for the Disadvantaged before that occurs."

A short silence descended as his cousin studied his unyielding expression. It was an expression that could cowl the most hearty soul. Unfortunately, Thorpe was blithely indifferent.

"Then what do you intend to do?"

Hart discovered himself reluctant to confess his rather nefarious plans. Odd considering his conscience had never been a troublesome beast. Still, he could not deny the most trifling sense of unease.

"I have it well in hand," he murmured.

"Of course." A rather sardonic smile touched Thorpe's lips as he continued to study Hart with a steady gaze. "What is she like?"

"Who?"

"Miss Conwell."

Hart gave a lift of his shoulder. "What is she like? She is a fortune hunter. What would you expect of someone of her ilk?"

"Ah, no doubt a hardened hag with the face of a hatchet and the body of a drowned rat? Or perhaps one of those mousy types who always stir the heart of elderly ladies?"

Hart could not halt his sharp bark of laughter. "You could not be further from the truth."

"She is beautiful?"

Hart dropped his gaze to study the cognac in his glass. "As beautiful as a Botticelli angel with eyes that lure a man to drown in their softness and a body that could tempt a saint to madness."

"Good God," Thorpe breathed. "I believe I shall have to make myself known to Miss Conwell."

A wholly irrational flare of annoyance raced through Hart at his cousin's casual words and he snapped his gaze back to the handsome countenance.

"You harbor a desire to be culled of your fortune?"

Thorpe merely smiled at the sharp question. "No, but I do harbor a very great desire for a Botticelli angel. Perhaps, unlike you, I shall consider her worth the cost."

Miss Conwell being seduced by this consummate rake?

Never.

The word surged through Hart's mind with shocking force and he shifted with a pang of discomfort. It was only that he was concerned for Thorpe, he hastily told himself. Molly Conwell would no doubt bleed him to his last quid. It was certainly not that he considered her delectable sweetness his own personal property.

On the point of warning his cousin to give a wide berth to Miss Conwell, Hart was abruptly distracted by a growing rumble of laughter and shouts from the outer rooms. Slowly rising to his feet, he glared toward the open door.

"What the devil is going on?" he muttered.

Thorpe also pressed himself upright, a hint of distaste upon his lean features. "No doubt a fight between the more reckless blades. Or a fool about to lose his entire inheritance upon a turn of the card."

Hart grimaced. London could be a dangerous place for young gentlemen with too much wealth and too little experience. He had seen far too many ruined before they could acquire the wisdom of maturity.

"Yes, no doubt," he agreed even as a tall, uniformed servant entered the room followed by a dozen boisterous noblemen upon his heel. His brows lifted at the unwelcome intrusion, and then he blinked in shock as he realized that the servant held a monkey attired in a ridiculous satin evening coat. "Good God above, what is going on?"

At his startled words, the servant gingerly lowered the monkey to the ground who promptly scrambled across the room to clutch at Hart's dove gray breeches.

"Miss Conwell requested that I deliver you this charming pet, along with the answer to your question."

Wondering if he had fallen asleep in his chair and stumbled into a nightmare, Hart gave a disbelieving shake of his head.

"What?"

"Yes, she does return the love you pledged with all her heart. And she would be honored to accept your gracious proposal of marriage."

A sudden cheer from the drunken onlookers filled the air as Hart gazed down in horror at the monkey attempting to tug the buckle from his shoe.

Why the devious, unscrupulous, conniving . . . wretch.

Clearly, she had decided to have a measure of revenge for this morning. And in the same stroke convince the entire male population of London that he had begged for her hand in marriage.

Bloody hell. He was going to throttle her.

But first he tilted back his head to laugh with rich amusement.

"Ah, the dubious delights of the theatre," the voluptuous, dark-haired Lady Falker muttered. "Where else can a lady of fashion be so easily preyed upon by the bolder rakes, her reputation shredded by the dragons, and her nerves in ever present danger of being dulled beyond repair by the portrayal of Hamlet by an actor as old and tedious as the play itself?"

Glancing about the ornate crimson and gold lobby of the theatre, Molly gave a faint chuckle. Unlike Georgie she had never enjoyed a London season, nor devoted her evenings to such frivolous pastimes. To her a visit to the theatre was a treat she fully intended to savor.

"Really, Georgie, I did not realize you held the theatre in such contempt," she murmured.

As if recalling Molly's stark lack of experience among society, Georgie wrinkled her nose in a charming manner.

"Forgive me, my dear. In truth my mood has little to do with the theatre. I have simply been bored and irritable of late."

Molly blinked in shock at her friend's confession. "How ever can you say such a thing?" she demanded. "You are young, beautiful and possess a life the rest of us poor females can only envy."

Something that might have been loneliness darkened the golden brown eyes before Georgie was snapping open the satin peach fan that perfectly matched her elegant gown.

"Perhaps. In any event I am quite pleased that you have come to stay with me. I have dearly missed your companionship."

Molly reached out to thread her arm through Georgie's as they moved up the marble steps. "And I yours."

"Of course, that does not mean that I fully approve of this dangerous game you seek to play with Lord Woodhart," Georgie murmured in low tones.

A sudden shock of unease slithered down Molly's spine, nearly making her stumble. Blast it all. She had badgered Georgie to come to the theatre tonight for the particular purpose of putting aside all thoughts of Lord Woodhart. After two days of pacing the floor and jumping at every knock upon the door, she could endure no more. If Hart intended to punish her for her rather impulsive and outlandish retaliation, then hiding in Georgie's elegant home would not halt him. Indeed, she very much feared that nothing would halt him.

"No more, Georgie," she said in what she hoped were decisive tones. "I have told you that my mind is quite set."

"Yes, I know, but that does not halt my concern." Glancing about the glittering crowd, Georgie leaned to speak directly into Molly's ear. "Lord Woodhart was already infuriated by his grandmother's will. I do not doubt he is ready for murder after you sent a monkey to his club."

A sudden heat touched Molly's cheeks. It had

no doubt been a wretchedly childish prank, but she had been beyond reasonable thought after he had treated her to such a public insult. She did, after all, possess some measure of pride.

"Trust me, Georgie, I do not intend to underestimate Lord Woodhart," she said wryly. "But neither do I intend to toss away the perfect opportunity to assist Andrew. This could be the answer to all my prayers."

"Fah." The beautiful widow gave a decidedly unladylike snort. "Really, Molly, that brother of yours should be . . ."

"No. I will not hear a word against Andrew," Molly sternly interrupted. Gads, one of these days she intended to lock the two of them in a chamber and not release them until they settled this ridiculous feud. "Whatever his faults he is the only family I possess. And I truly believe that he has learned his lesson."

"For heaven's sake, you have always been ridiculously naive when it comes to your brother."

"Please, Georgie, I do not wish to argue."

She could feel her companion stiffen before Georgie was at last heaving a faint sigh. "Neither do I. Shall we take our seats?"

With the ease of a skilled navigator, Lady Falker plotted a course through the mingling crowd, ruthlessly deflecting those gentlemen who sought to gain her attention, and assiduously avoiding those matrons who could not be readily dismissed. Eagerly absorbing the tingling excitement that filled the air and the elegant opulence of her surroundings, Molly allowed herself to be steered to the small box toward the back of the theatre. Once within Georgie heaved a sigh of relief and dropped onto one of the delicate seats, pulling Molly down next to her.

"Thank goodness we escaped before Lady Oberman could capture us," Georgie muttered. "She considers her very distant connection to my late husband as carte blanche to forever badger me with complaints of my independent manner, my choice of gowns, my friends and even my servants. It is little wonder her three sons have chosen to flee to India. Were she my mother I would have been forced to gag and bind her in the cellar long ago."

Molly smiled in sympathy. Having encountered Lady Oberman, she had to admit that her friend was indeed cursed with a most unpleasant relative.

"I have always believed that a good, stout cellar is essential when one is cursed with a number of unwelcome relatives," she agreed.

"Indeed." Casting an absent glance about the rapidly filling seats, Georgie gave a small jerk as her gaze lingered upon a box situated near the grand stage. "Oh dear."

"What is it?"

Georgie turned to meet Molly's curious expression. "It appears that your dutiful fiancé has decided to make a rare appearance in society."

"Hart?" Molly felt a chill of dismay fill her heart. "Where?"

"In his family box." Georgie discreetly tilted her head in the direction of the lavish box across the way. "Complete with another woman."

It took only a moment for Molly to discover

her treacherous fiancé. Her heart nearly halted as she studied his male form attired in stark black with a crimson waistcoat. Dash it all, but he was magnificent as he sprawled with negligent ease in his chair, the candlelight warming his pale skin and adding a satin sheen to his raven curls. There was not another gentleman in the theatre that could compare to his fierce, elegant beauty. Perhaps not in all of London.

But then he slowly shifted to whisper in the ear of his companion and Molly was brought abruptly back to her senses.

Her eyes narrowed as she swept a condemning glance over the titian-haired beauty who was attired in a gown that was a certain invitation to lung fever. Indeed, Molly was not at all certain that there was more than a token effort to cover the ample bosom that was deliberately thrust toward Hart. An obvious tart, she told herself. But one with the sort of beauty that was bound to stir the attention of gentlemen. Certainly every male gaze in the room was currently fixed upon her.

"Who is she?" Molly demanded.

"She goes simply by the name of Celeste," Georgie reluctantly revealed. "Rumor has it that she is the most expensive courtesan in London."

Well, at least the beast appeared to possess excellent taste, she wryly told herself.

"I see."

Next to her, Georgie slowly opened her fan and waved it in an absent fashion. "It is odd. Lord Woodhart has always been a renowned rake, but he has never openly flaunted his numerous mistresses. Indeed, he has always been known for his discretion."

Molly lifted her brows in surprise. "Discretion? Why he jilted poor Miss Darlington at the altar." She recalled her friend to the disgrace that had shocked all of society near four years ago. "That is a far cry from discreet."

"True enough, but over the past few years he has gone to great lengths to avoid having his name connected with any woman." She shot Molly a speculative glance. "Which begs the question of why he would part with his usual habits on this evening."

A rush of anger flared through Molly. It did not take a great deal of intelligence to realize precisely why Lord Woodhart would suddenly discover the need to flaunt his beautiful mistress.

"No doubt in the hopes of embarrassing me," she gritted. "After all, the rumors that we are engaged are already making their way through town. No doubt he thinks to humiliate me by appearing with his mistress at the same night that I am in attendance."

Georgie gave a flick of her fan. "But how did he know you would be in attendance?"

Yes, how did he know? It was not as if a crier walked the streets informing all and sundry of her plans. Molly pursed her lips in thought before giving a faint shrug of her shoulders. One vexing annoyance at a time, she ruefully decided.

"I will soon enough discover," she swore, her gaze lingering upon that warrior profile. "For now, however, I must consider what is to be done with my treacherous cad of a fiancé."

"You could always indulge in a delicious scene," Georgie suggested in low tones.

"I fear that is precisely what he is hoping for."

"What?"

With more effort than she cared to acknowledge, Molly wrenched her attention from the gentleman across the theatre to meet her friend's puzzled gaze.

"Do you not see? For the moment Lord Woodhart has no reasonable means of contesting his grandmother's will. But, if I were to prove I were somehow unhinged or unsuitable to take the place as Viscountess Woodhart, then I do not doubt he would easily discover a judge willing to abolish my claim upon my inheritance. I cannot risk having an ugly scandal attached to my name."

Georgie wrinkled her nose in resigned agreement. "So you intend to do nothing?"

Molly paused. She could leave, of course. Or remain and pretend that she did not note that the gentleman who had presumably pledged his loyalty to her was currently mooning over another woman. A woman moreover who did not even possess the decency to cover all her parts properly.

Both choices, however, would ensure that by tomorrow morning she would be the source of spiteful amusement throughout London.

No. She could not bear that. It was simply not in her nature to meekly turn the other cheek. At least not when it came to bloody Lord Woodhart.

"Actually I believe I should join Hart and congratulate him on his fortune in claiming the attention of such a beautiful woman."

Georgie gave a choked cough of disbelief. "Have you gone daft, Molly? You will be the talk of the town if you enter that box."

A determined expression hardened Molly's countenance. "It is obvious that Hart has already ensured that I will be the talk of the town."

"Perhaps, but . . ."

"Listen to me, Georgie, I can either remain here and allow myself to be a pathetic source of amusement"—Molly surged to her feet, ignoring the absurd manner in which her knees trembled—"or, I can reveal that I am utterly indifferent to my fiancé's obvious disdain."

"Oh, lord." Georgie gave a slow shake of her head. "This is bound to be a disaster."

"Trust me, Georgie."

Chapter Four

Even as Hart played the role of the skilled seducer, he was acutely aware of the moment Miss Molly Conwell entered the theatre. It was in the manner that his skin tingled with sudden awareness, and his heart added an additional beat. He could almost convince himself that he could feel the burning touch of her velvet brown eyes and catch the scent of sweet lavender.

A rather annoying whimsy, despite the fact that he had been impatiently awaiting her arrival. He was uncertain that he desired to be quite so responsive to a female he claimed to detest. Especially when he was utterly impervious to the woman seated so closely at his side. A woman considered to be the most beautiful, talented courtesan in all of England.

Hart shifted closer to Celeste, attempting to thrust aside his odd fancies. He even reached out a lazy finger to trace the line of her plunging bodice. Soon enough he would have Miss Conwell fleeing London.

Then he could put all thoughts of her behind him, he told himself.

Well . . . perhaps not completely behind him,

he amended with an unwitting smile. She was, after all, responsible for the thoroughly disreputable monkey currently running amok in his household. Although it was an ill-mannered beast, Hart had discovered himself unable to toss the creature into the street despite the fact his servants were in near mutiny.

He found the monkey a source of amusement; he had informed his housekeeper of as much when she threatened to walk out the door. There was nothing more to it than that.

"You are comfortable, I trust, my beauty?" he at last forced himself to murmur, knowing that he could not continue to sit there in rather daft silence.

Celeste gave her curls a practiced toss even as she regarded him with a sultry warmth. "As comfortable as I can be with every gaze upon us."

"Ah, but surely you are accustomed to attracting such notice? You are extraordinarily lovely," he gallantly murmured.

She smiled, but there was a rather disconcerting glitter in the slanted green eyes. "I fear I cannot quite comprehend why you wished to come to the theatre, my lord."

Hart offered a negligent shrug, not at all prepared to confess the truth. He did not believe the courtesan would be particularly pleased to discover she was only at his side to embarrass his fiancée.

"To strike envy in the heart of every gentleman in London, of course."

He expected her to purr at his flippant words. Instead her gaze merely narrowed. "Very pretty, but I well know that you have no need or desire for notoriety. Every gentleman in London already envies you. Our evening could be much better spent alone. My . . . skills are better suited to a private setting."

Hart readily believed her husky claim. From all reports Celeste was without peer in the world of debauchery. Unfortunately at the moment, he was not in a debauching mood. Not when his attention was determinedly centered upon the treacherous angel across the theatre.

"Later, my beauty."

She reached up to stroke his hand that still lay against her bodice. "You have promised that since you so unexpectedly called upon me. I begin to wonder what it truly is you desire from me, Hart."

He bent his head to stroke his lips over her cheek even as he covertly glanced toward the distant box. "A few hours of your time."

"Why?"

"I should think that would be obvious."

"I thought it was. Now I begin to wonder."

"I . . ." Abruptly realizing that Lady Falker was now seated alone in her box, Hart straightened with a frown. "Where the devil did she go?"

"Is something the matter, my lord?"

"Nothing that need trouble you," he muttered, his brows drawn together. Had Molly fled the theatre? It did not seem at all in keeping with her stubborn temperament. Indeed, he had presumed that she would rather roast in the netherworld than reveal that he had managed to injure her pride. Still, there was no mistaking the fact that she was no longer seated next to her companion.

Hart determinedly attempted to stir a measure of pleasure. This was precisely what he desired. Molly would soon be a source of pity and amusement throughout London. An unbearable situation for any woman.

"Really, Hart, you are the most provoking gentleman," Celeste protested at his side. "I am unaccustomed to being treated with such obvious disregard."

Reluctantly turning to regard the exquisite countenance now marred with a frown, Hart bit back a sigh of frustration. With Molly now suitably put into her place, he could no doubt devote the rest of his evening to pleasure. All sorts of delicious, wicked pleasure. Unfortunately, he discovered it annoyingly difficult to concentrate upon the beautiful courtesan.

"Forgive me." He conjured a smile. "I fear I am rather distracted this evening."

The courtesan's expression was decidedly knowing. "Who is she?"

"I beg your pardon?"

Celeste laughed softly at his wary expression. "I was not allowed the formal education of your fine lady acquaintances, my lord, but I do comprehend all there is to know of gentlemen. The only thing that could possibly distract you from me is another woman."

He gave a discomforted cough. Blast. He could hardly argue the truth of her accusation. It was most certainly another woman distracting him.

Although not in the manner she suspected. Or at least, not entirely in the manner she suspected.

"Celeste, I . . ."

His soft apology was never completed as the curtain to the box was unexpectedly thrust open and a slender golden-haired angel swept toward his seat.

"Hart, what a lovely surprise. I did not know you would be here this evening."

Rising to his feet, Hart swept his gaze over the woman who was supposed to be cowering in shame. Grudgingly, he conceded that she appeared remarkably pretty in the soft rose gown with her hair in a braided knot that allowed several wisps of gold to brush her ivory skin. Not even the militant glitter in the dark eyes managed to dim her glow of sweet innocence. And that scent . . .

Abruptly realizing that he was actually leaning forward to catch a whiff of her lavender aroma, Hart sternly stiffened his spine. Dash it all. This woman was the enemy. If he desired to be sniffing at a woman, he possessed a perfectly trained courtesan who was ready and decidedly willing.

With a well-practiced effort, Hart forced himself to adopt his normal air of casual nonchalance as he peered down his nose at the audacious chit.

"Molly."

She flipped open her ivory fan as she regarded him with a stiff smile. "Why did you not tell me you were coming to the theatre, you naughty boy? Poor Georgiana will be so vexed with you."

Hart's brows slowly lifted. He was not certain what he had expected. Shrill accusations. A slap to the face. Even being pushed over the edge of the railing. Certainly not this brittle charm.

"Will she?"

"Oh, yes." She moved toward him in a coy fashion. "She abhors such a crush, but I simply could not come by myself."

"Indeed? I begin to wonder if there is nothing you will not dare," he mocked in dark tones.

Her chin thrust upward. "Very little, you will discover."

She had no need to convince him, Hart acknowledged with a wry flare of amusement. He was beginning to suspect she possessed more foolish courage and sheer daring than any person he had ever before encountered.

Gads, what other woman would have brazenly approached him when he was in full public view with his mistress?

He folded his arms over his chest. "Perhaps you did not notice, my love, but I am rather occupied at the moment."

The dark eyes flashed before she was rigidly resuming her air of insouciance. "How could I not notice such a lovely companion? Will you not introduce us?"

"Introduce . . .?" His brows snapped together. For God's sake, did the woman have no decency? "No. I blasted will not introduce you. It would hardly be proper."

"Oh, fudge. What is a bit of impropriety between us, Hart?" she taunted as she gave a saucy toss of her head and turned toward the woman watching them in speculative silence. "Good evening, I am Miss Conwell, Hart's fiancée."

The famous green eyes widened as Celeste glanced toward Hart's stony features. "Fiancée?"

"Yes, indeed," Molly plunged heedless onward, either oblivious or impervious to the sudden silence that had descended upon the theatre. "Is that not so, my dear?"

He gave a lift of one broad shoulder. "If you wish to make the claim."

"But of course I do. What woman would not desire to claim a gentleman of such noble virtue, such unwavering integrity, and such obvious morality?"

"No doubt a wise one," he purred, not at all certain how he could be so bloody furious and yet so amused at the same moment.

"Well, we have already ascertained that I have never been particularly wise," Molly murmured, and then as the curtain upon the stage began to rattle open, she audaciously moved to plant herself in the seat he had just vacated. "Ah, I believe the performance is about to commence."

Hart snapped his brows together. "You cannot remain here."

"Why ever not? Although I would never wound Georgie's tender sensibilities the view from your box is far superior. I promise I shall not trouble you a wit."

"Molly," Hart gritted.

"Yes, Hart?"

"I would like a word with you in private."

"At the intermission, my love," she promised with an airy wave of her hand.

A taut silence descended until there was suddenly a rustle of heavy silk and Celeste moved toward the back of the box. With swift movements, Hart was crossing to block her retreat.

"You are not leaving?" he demanded in low tones.

Expecting her to be infuriated by the ridiculous situation, Hart was startled when he realized that the green eyes were glittering with a wicked amusement.

"Unlike you, my lord, I know when I have been clearly routed." She gave an elegant lift of her shoulder. "Besides which, I make a point of never appearing so close to a woman younger than myself. It is hardly good for business."

Hart grimaced, knowing that he was not nearly as disappointed at having the beautiful Impure slip from his grasp as he should be. In truth, it was rather a relief to know he would not be forced to invent some flimsy excuse for why he would not be spending the night in her charming arms.

"I will have my coach take you home."

Her expression became wry. "Do not bother. I shall have no difficulties in discovering another to take your place."

"No, I suppose not," he murmured, reaching out to take her hand and lift it to his lips. "Forgive me."

Unexpectedly, she pulled her fingers free to lightly stroke his cheek. "Save your pity for yourself, Hart. I have a feeling you will need it."

Despite her most fervent efforts, Molly discovered she was unable to make out more than a low mutter of conversation behind her. Was Hart attempting to convince the beauty to remain? He could not, after all, be particularly pleased to have his evening of wicked debauchery brought to such an abrupt and unpleasant end. Even if he was merely using the courtesan to rid himself of an unwanted fiancée.

Or perhaps Celeste was attempting to convince Hart to leave with her . . .

A sudden ball of dread lodged in her stomach.

Good heavens. She had not considered the possibility that her fiancé might simply abandon her in the box while he openly left with his mistress.

If he truly desired to humiliate her, there could be no more effective means. Why society would no doubt talk of the crushing blow for years to come.

Gripping her fan so tightly that the delicate ivory threatened to snap, Molly heard the curtain at the back of the box slide open. She even forgot to breath until at last the sound of footsteps drawing inexorably closer could be detected over the wild beat of her heart.

So, he had not left. Only then did she manage to suck in a measure of air to her tight lungs. Air that was swiftly lost when warm, male fingers gripped her bare neck in a firm, unshakable grasp.

"Are you certain you desire to sit so close to the edge, my love?" he whispered, bending until his lips brushed her ear. "I would not desire to have you tumble over the edge."

Firmly telling herself that the warm flutters in

the pit of her stomach had nothing to do with his lingering touch, nor the soft brush of his lips, Molly stiffened her spine.

"Oh, I would not fear, my lord. I would only return."

"Rather like the plague, hmm?"

"A hardly flattering comparison for your fiancée," she muttered. "No wonder your rather tawdry companion felt the need to flee with such haste."

"Tawdry." His low chuckle seemed to pour directly down her spine. Worse, those disturbing fingers had softened their grip until he was gently stroking the tender skin of her neck. "Do I detect a note of jealousy?"

"Certainly not," she denied, her tones ridiculously unsteady. Then, as she realized that not even a stark raving fool would believe she was indifferent toward the strikingly beautiful courtesan, she gave a restless shrug. "No, that is not entirely true. I cannot imagine there is any woman who would not envy such beauty. It is only a pity that she has been forced to trade upon her loveliness to survive."

Behind her Molly could feel Hart stiffen, as if caught off guard by her reluctant confession. Slowly, he withdrew his hands and moved to take the seat next to her. He did not, however, make any attempt to appear as if he were interested in the actors who were even now moving about the stage. Instead he turned to fully face her, his arm casually draped over the back of his gilt-edged chair.

"Celeste appears content enough."

Molly turned her head to encounter his gaze that was unnervingly piercing. Despite the vast crowd, many of whom were no doubt avidly watching their exchange, they might have been alone in the shadowed box. A rather disturbing sensation.

Still, she could not afford to reveal any hint of unease. Not to Hart, or the jaded members of the *ton*.

"Because she is paid to seem content," she retorted in a thankfully firm tone. "I do not believe any woman can be happy offering herself to an endless string of gentlemen."

"Morals from you, Molly?" he lightly mocked.

"Sympathy, my lord. I happen to know what it is like to be alone and forced to fend for oneself. A woman possesses few choices. If not for your grandmother, I do not know what would have become of me."

His features hardened at her words. "If you hope to stir my softer emotions, my love, let me assure you that I have none."

She rolled her eyes at the vast understatement. He might as well have reminded her that the sky was blue. "Of course not. You are the Heartless Viscount, after all."

"Precisely."

"You appear to take great pleasure in your reputation," she retorted with an unwitting frown. "I presume you must enjoy being feared."

"It is preferable to having others presume me to be a fool."

"Ah, yes. Everyone must be out to take advantage of you, eh Hart?"

He deliberately allowed his gaze to sweep over

her slender form, lingering for a moment upon her soft lips.

"Enough that I have learned to protect myself."

The insult was as subtle as a slap to the face, but Molly refused to rise to the obvious bait. Instead she slowly tilted her head to one side.

"How lonely you must be."

"Lonely?"

"A gentleman who never trusts another must always be lonely."

He stiffened, almost as if she had hit a vulnerable nerve, but before she could be certain he was stretching out his legs and returning to his façade of impenetrable ease.

"I manage to muddle along."

"Yes, but are you happy?"

His gaze narrowed. "Are you?"

Molly bit her lip at the swift rejoinder. Of course she was not happy. Her brother was in mortal danger. She was forced to deceive and challenge a gentleman who disturbed her in a manner she found difficult to comprehend. And the peaceful existence she had always dreamed of at Oakgrove seemed to grow ever more distant with each passing day.

It was rather ironic really. Unlike many of her friends, she had never rebelled against the future that was expected of a young lady of society. She did not long for adventures or daring flirtations. She did not particularly desire to travel about the world or be the toast of the Season. All she wanted was a husband who would treat her with kindness and respect and a family to call her own.

Simple dreams, and yet she might as well have wished for the moon.

"*Touché,*" she muttered.

Hart stilled, searching her pale countenance with a searing intensity. And then, as if not entirely pleased with his inner thoughts, he gave a faint shake of his head.

"Tell me, how did you meet my grandmother?" he abruptly demanded.

"I met her at a charity tea that I was attending with Georgie," she readily answered. And why should she not? She had nothing nefarious to hide. Well, at least not in her dealings with Lady Woodhart, she silently amended. "She claimed that she had been great friends with my grandmother in her youth and asked me to visit her at her home. I believe she enjoyed reminiscing of her younger days."

"And you, of course, pretended a vast enjoyment in such reminisces?"

"There was no pretense." Molly met his gaze squarely. Whatever this man's suspicions, her love for Lady Woodhart had been utterly genuine. "I very much enjoyed hearing of my grandmother's youthful antics. Not all of us are so jaded and cynical as you."

He slowly leaned forward, his eyes glittering in the shadowed light. "I should not be so cynical if you had not insinuated your way into my grandmother's household."

She itched to rap her fan against his skull. Thankfully, it was her favorite fan and she was not about to have it broken upon thick granite.

"Lady Woodhart desired a companion and I

was in need of employment. There was nothing deceitful about the arrangement."

"And why would the sister of a Baron be in need of employment?"

Molly's heart nearly stuttered to a stop at the unexpected attack. Although she had learned to deflect even the most pressing questions concerning her brother, she discovered herself shifting uneasily in her seat. Hart was not at all like others. Not only did he possess a shrewd intelligence, but he was also a relentless opponent. If he sensed even the smallest hint of suspicion in regard to Andrew, then he would not halt until he possessed every sordid detail of the truth.

"My family has always been in financial straits, as I am sure you must be aware," she at last managed to retort between stiff lips.

"And yet according to rumor your brother is living quite splendidly, if rather reclusively, somewhere in Europe. Does he not see that you are provided for?"

"I . . . prefer to remain independent."

Hart made a sound of disapproval deep in his throat. "So, your worthless fribble of a brother has abandoned you and to recover the position lost to you, you conceived a plot to use my grandmother to restore you to the life of luxury."

His condemning words should not have troubled her. She had heard such accusations from him endless times over the past months. But oddly she found herself batting back ridiculous tears.

No doubt it was simply her frustration at having her brother so ruthlessly disparaged without being allowed to defend him, she told herself sternly. It could have nothing to do with his seething dislike toward her. Or his determined insistence to believe the worse in her.

"Believe what you will, my lord."

"Oh, I intend to."

Realizing that she was actually trembling with the force of her emotions, Molly abruptly rose to her feet. She had accomplished what she had set out to do. Whatever the whispers tomorrow, they would not speak of her humiliation, or of Hart's disdain for his fiancée.

"If you will excuse me, I believe that I will return to Georgie."

He lifted himself upright, his hand reaching out to grasp her arm. "I thought that you claimed I possessed a superior box?"

"Superior, perhaps," she muttered, determinedly drawing her arm from his grip. "But there is a rather foul stench in the air. Good night, my lord."

Chapter Five

Molly chose the back parlor after awaking late and breaking her fast upon toast and tea. It was not that she was hiding, she reassured herself sternly. Or avoiding any visitors that might stray past Lady Falker's lovely home, though in truth her sleepless night had left her in rather an ill humor.

It was quite simply that she preferred a measure of privacy when she worked upon her charcoal sketches.

On the whole Molly was remarkably modest. She did not believe her pale features and golden hair possessed more than a passable beauty. She had never thought herself above moderate intelligence. And the inner strength that had allowed her to survive after her brother's foolish disaster she considered more a consequence of necessity than any true gift.

But she did harbor a vanity when it came to her sketches. She had always possessed a talent for capturing a scene or countenance with a stark honesty. Most would say too much honesty. She made no attempt to shadow or soften. Nor did she seek only beauty to capture. Instead she sought to evoke the feeling of the moment: happiness, terror, sadness, loss.

At the moment, she was concentrating upon a maid she had witnessed standing beside the mews early that morning. For some reason the servant's covert manner as she had huddled within the thick ivy had caught Molly's fancy. There had been something very furtive in her expression, as if she were hoping to slip from her duties unnoted, or even to meet her lover on the sly.

Barely noting the vague rustlings of the busy household, Molly fully lost herself within her bold strokes, capturing the expression of half dread and half elation that had illuminated the rather plain countenance. It was not until the door to the parlor was abruptly tossed open that she reluctantly set aside her charcoal and turned to confront her friend.

In elegant style, Georgie was attired in a deep jade gown that emphasized the purity of her white skin and the silky gloss of her dark curls. Surrounded by the rich ivory and gold furnishings, she appeared every inch a lady of refined fashion. A far cry from the hoydenish young girl that had once preferred fishing and climbing trees to being a proper maiden, Molly thought with an inward smile.

"Well, you have done it, my dear," she announced in dramatic tones, her eyes sparkling with excitement.

Giving a blink of bewilderment, Molly wiped her fingers upon a damp cloth. "I suppose that is wonderful; however, I have not the faintest notion of what it is that I have done."

Georgie laughed as she swayed across the Parisian carpet. "All of town is speaking of your daring at the theatre last evening."

"Oh." Molly grimaced as she tossed aside the cloth. Throughout the endless night she had recalled every moment of her time with Hart. The suspicion in the dark eyes, the edge in his voice, the threat of his coiled body. But oddly, it was the memory of the aching pleasure of his touch that had kept her pacing the floor. Blast it all. "And what do they say?"

"That the Heartless Viscount has at last met his match."

Molly lifted her brows before abruptly tilting her head back to laugh with disbelief. If only they knew. They would not be nearly so impressed if they realized that it was sheer desperation, along with a large dose of foolishness that prompted her daring deeds.

"I wish I could be so confident."

Georgie's smile slowly faded as she regarded her friend with a measure of concern. "You are having second thoughts?"

"And third and fourth."

Stepping closer, her friend reached out to grasp Molly's hand in a firm grip. "There is no need to go through this, Molly."

She gave a slow shake of her head. "Unfortunately there is every need. And I am determined to see it through."

"I could just throttle Andrew for this."

Georgie's pretty features flushed with the force of her emotions. "If it were not for him . . ."

Molly sternly stepped back, her own countenance hard with determination. "No more, Georgie. I have warned you that I will not have you speaking ill of Andrew."

Georgie battled her inner demons before at last heaving a rueful sigh. "Oh, very well."

"Thank you."

With an obvious effort to restore her earlier good humor, the dark-haired beauty summoned a smile. "Instead let us decide what we shall do today. Although society is rather thin there are always any number of entertainments. What do you say we have luncheon and make our plans?"

Under normal circumstances, Molly would have been delighted to devote her day to exploring London and enjoying the intellectual salons that she had only dreamed of attending. But these were far from normal circumstances. Wherever she might go, she would always be on guard. How could she possibly relax when she would know that Hart might be lurking about every corner?

Still, she could not remain forever cowering in Georgie's home. Not only would she go mad from boredom, but she could not bear the thought of appearing the coward.

"If you wish," she conceded.

Before Georgie could respond the door to the parlor was once again pushed open. On this occasion it was the dignified butler who entered and offered a stiff bow.

"Pardon me, my lady, but Lord Woodhart has

arrived and is desirous of speaking with Miss Conwell."

Molly clapped a hand to her suddenly heaving stomach. Dear lord, she had not expected him to actually make an appearance at the elegant townhouse. Not unless it was to throttle her in her sleep.

"Hart is here?"

"Yes, miss. In the front parlor."

"How dare he?" Georgie muttered, turning toward Molly with a decided flounce. "We can easily send him on his way, Molly. There is no need to speak with him."

It was tempting. She would dearly love to witness the arrogant intruder tossed from the house. Oh, it would no doubt take several burly footmen, and perhaps a large stick, but it would surely be worth the mayhem.

Then her pesky common sense returned and she heaved a sigh. There would no doubt be a measure of satisfaction in knowing she had bested the annoying gentleman, but it would only be fleeting. If she had learned nothing else of Lord Woodhart, she did know that he was quite the most stubborn of beasts.

"I fear he would only return, Georgie," she murmured.

"Then we can send him on his way again."

Her lips twitched at her friend's haughty tone. At the moment, she sounded every bit Lady Falker.

"A most pleasant notion; however, he is quite capable of provoking an unpleasant scene in public if I refuse to meet with him," she retorted with a wry smile. "I prefer whatever he might have to say be in private."

Georgie frowned. "You are certain?"

Molly paused before giving a nod of her head. "Yes. He can hardly do away with me in your front parlor."

"Fah. I would put nothing beyond Lord Wood-hart."

"All will be well."

Molly reached out to squeeze her friend's hand before squaring her shoulders and following the rigid servant out of the room and down the long corridor toward the front of the townhouse.

Absently, she noted the marble statues set in shallow alcoves and the various landscapes that Lord Falker had acquired during his long life-time. But for once she did not halt to admire the numerous treasures that Georgie took so much for granted. Instead she battled the nearly over-whelming urge to flee to her bedchamber and barricade the door.

Blast. She could not imagine what had brought Hart to the townhouse. Well, beyond the obvious desire for murder.

Did he think to intimidate her? To threaten her? To toss her over his shoulder and haul her to the nearest cliff?

"No. He cannot harm you Molly Conwell," she muttered to herself. "Nor can he bully you unless you allow it."

Somewhat reassured, she smoothed the skirts of her pale lavender gown as the butler pulled open the door to the front parlor and she was left with nothing to do but sweep past him into the pretty room with yellow satin wall panels and pale green furnishings.

Determined to appear indifferent to his unexpected intrusion, she refused to allow her steps to falter, at least not until the large male form stepped from the shadows near the bay window and offered an elegant bow.

Her mouth went dry as she regarded his smoke gray coat and silver waistcoat that he had matched with black breeches. Bathed in the spring sunlight his countenance possessed a chiseled perfection, his eyes shimmering with a restless intelligence. Gads but he was so damnably . . . magnificent, she inanely acknowledged. From the glossy raven curls to the tips of his Hessians, he possessed a powerful beauty that was enough to make any maiden's knees go weak.

Even a maiden who thoroughly detested him.

Pressing her hands together, she forced herself to ignore the distinctly unwelcome awareness that shivered over her skin.

"You wished to speak with me, my lord?" she demanded, quite pleased when her voice did not come out in a squeak.

There was a moment of silence as he regarded her, his gaze oddly intense as he surveyed her pale countenance. Almost as if it had been weeks rather than hours since they had last encountered one another.

"I have brought the remainder of your belongings," he at last said, his hand waving toward the valise set upon a distant sofa.

Molly frowned in decided puzzlement. "There

was no need to bring them yourself. A servant could easily have delivered the case."

His lips twisted in a dry smile. "And deprive me of the opportunity to spend a few moments in the company of my beloved fiancée? Do not be absurd."

Her spine stiffened at his mocking tone. Not that she was in any way surprised. He had already made it painfully clear he intended to make this faux engagement as difficult as possible. Understandable perhaps, but decidedly unpleasant.

"What is it you want, my lord?" she demanded.

"A rather dangerous question."

"Beyond having my head upon a platter," she clarified in dry tones.

Without warning he prowled forward, not halting until he was towering over her in a most disconcerting fashion.

"It is not a matter of what I want. But rather upon what you want, Miss Conwell."

Grudgingly tilting back her head, Molly forced herself to squarely meet the glittering black gaze. "I beg your pardon?"

"What is your price, my dear?" he demanded. "What will it take to put an end to this ludicrous situation?"

Abruptly, she understood. He had not managed to humiliate her as he had hoped. Or at least not thoroughly enough to make her flee in horror. Now he was forced to once again return to plain intimidation.

It was fortunate for her that she had been raised in a household with the sort of gentleman who used such tactics upon a regular basis. She had learned long ago how to stand her ground.

Taking a step back so that she did not have to crane her neck, Molly folded her arms over her chest.

"The truth, my lord?"

He narrowed his gaze at her chilled tones. "If you are capable of uttering something that vaguely resembles the truth."

"There is nothing you can offer me."

A sharp silence descended as his arrogant nose flared in anger. "And what does that mean?"

She gave a negligent lift of her shoulder. "I do not consider our engagement ludicrous."

"You must be mad," he accused tightly. "You do not desire to be my wife. And I assure you I would rather be drawn and quartered than even consider the possibility of you ever becoming Lady Woodhart."

Drawn and quartered? Well. That was rather . . . explicit.

Heaven help any woman foolish enough to truly desire Hart as a husband, she wryly concluded. As far as fiancés went, he was most certainly a wretched specimen.

"It was your grandmother's desire. I must respect her wishes."

"Fah. And what of mine?"

"No one can force you to the chapel, my lord." She carefully edged back another step. It seemed rather sensible to be out of easy reach as his eyes darkened with frustrated anger. "If you do not desire to wed me then there is nothing to compel you to do so."

"Nothing but thirty thousand pounds."

"A rather meaningless sum to you, I should think."

The warrior features tightened in a dangerous manner. "Is that what you tell yourself to ease your conscience?"

Molly felt herself stiffen at the unexpected thrust. Dash it all. She did not want to consider her conscience. Not at least until Andrew was safe. Until then she could not bear to dwell upon her less than honorable behavior.

"My conscience does not need any easing," she forced herself to lie in light tones. "I never sought nor demanded anything of Lady Woodhart."

The dark gaze flicked a condemning glance over her rigid body. "Ah, but you are ready enough to grasp a fortune when it is offered."

"I have told you, I am merely complying with your grandmother's last request."

"Of course." He offered a disbelieving snort. "And you are perfectly content to become my wife?"

"I would not say content. More . . . resigned."

For a moment he glared deep into her eyes, almost as if seeking to break her spirit with the mere force of his will. Then, as if sensing she was not about to be easily bullied, he at last stepped back and sucked in a deep breath.

"Very well."

Molly regarded him with a wary gaze. She did not like that air of resolve that suddenly hardened about his large form.

"If that is all, I should return to Georgie."

Far from attempting to halt her, Hart instead

offered an elegant bow. "That is all, for the moment. But rest assured that we shall be seeing each other very soon, my love. Indeed you may depend upon it."

"No, no. Far too dull." Shrugging off the offending coat, Hart glanced in the mirror at the short, wafer thin valet with a shock of silver hair who stood behind him with a sour expression. "Perhaps the blue with silver stitching, Carter."

The sourness only deepened at Hart's request. "My lord, you have already disdained the blue with silver stitching as being too frivolous."

"Have I?"

"Yes, as well as the claret for being too gaudy, the black for being too somber, the gray for having ridiculous buttons, the green . . ."

Hart held up a slender hand with a sudden chuckle. As a rule he was not a demanding employer. Oh, certainly he possessed a few odd quirks. He demanded that his boots possess the gloss of polished glass. He demanded a hot bath with the scent of sandalwood the moment he awoke, and his meals served in the comfort of his library rather than the grand dining room. But overall he preferred to tend to his own needs without an army of servants constantly underfoot.

"I take your point, Carter," he retorted in wry tones. "Clearly I shall have to have a word with my tailor. He seems to have burdened me with an entire wardrobe of unsuitable coats."

The servant gave a lift of his gray brows.

"Perhaps if you were to offer me your plans for this evening I could assist in choosing the proper attire."

Hart's expression hardened as he met his servant's curious gaze in the mirror. "My plans are quite simple. I intend to terrify my sweet fiancée into flight."

Carter gave a discreet cough. It was the closest he had ever come to revealing surprise in the near ten years he had been in Hart's employ.

"Beg pardon, sir?"

"It is quite simple, Carter. Miss Conwell has made it obvious that she will not be bribed, bullied, nor humiliated into giving up her ridiculous game. The only option left is to terrify her into conceding defeat."

"I see." There was the faintest hint of disapproval in the smooth tones. "And how do you intend to terrify her, my lord?"

Hart's lips twitched. "Do not regard me in that censorious fashion, Carter. As tempting as it might be to have her tossed into the Thames I have always considered any sort of violence toward women as reprehensible. I intend nothing more nefarious than becoming her most devoted suitor."

The brows rose even higher. "Forgive me, but is that not more likely to win her heart?"

"If she possessed a heart." Hart briefly allowed himself to consider Miss Molly Conwell. He intended to dwell upon her black soul, and greed-riddled heart, but instead the image of her countenance and slender frame rose to mind. Not only rose to mind, but with surprising ease and in shocking detail. From the precise shade of gold in her curls to the manner her sweet curves filled out her muslin gowns. He gave an abrupt shake of his head. Gads, she must be driving him batty. "Thankfully, Miss Conwell is without the more tender sentiments of most ladies. She is quite convinced that I shall balk at arriving at the chapel and leave her free to claim her fortune. If I convince her that I fully intend to make her my wife, nothing will induce her to continue with this charade."

Carter gently cleared his throat, as if not overly impressed with Hart's latest scheme. "And if she does continue?"

His gaze narrowed. "Then I shall consider more drastic measures."

There was no mistaking the determination in his tones and the valet gave a slow nod of his head. "Very good, sir. Shall we see about the wine coat with gold buttons?"

"Perfect."

Standing in the shadows of Lady Hulford's ivory and gold salon, Hart watched his prey with a lazy gaze.

He supposed he should be angry. Not only had his scheme to shame Miss Molly Conwell into giving up this absurd engagement failed, but she had once again stubbornly stood up to his attempts at intimidation.

Oddly however, he was not nearly as disappointed at having to change his tactics and continue the game as he should be.

Well, perhaps not entirely odd. His lips twitched as he watched her move through the dull crowd.

Even at a distance, Molly managed to appear startlingly beautiful in a pale pink gown with her golden curls threaded with satin roses. Indeed, she was utterly delectable. It was little surprise that any number of male gazes were trained upon her slender form with a decided hint of hunger.

Whatever her sins, and they were numerous, she was a beautiful and desirable woman. Why the devil should he not enjoy teasing her in such a pleasurable manner?

If he could taste of her sweetness and at the same time ensure that she learned a stern lesson in attempting to steal from him, so much the better.

Slowly straightening from the wall, Hart began to circle the room. He was too wise to take a direct path to his victim. For the moment Molly was unaware of his presence at the tedious gathering. It seemed preferable to catch her off guard rather than be forced to chase her through the milling throng.

Avoiding the clutch of fluttering debutantes near the refreshment table and the ever-dangerous dragons that lurked near the potted palms, he at last threaded his way to the fluted columns. Only when he was standing directly behind his treacherous fiancée did he come to a halt and gently reach out to run his fingers lightly over the bare skin of her shoulder.

Immediately outraged by the intimate touch, Molly whirled about, her eyes widening as she realized precisely who was making such a bold overture.

"Hart," she breathed in dismay.

"Good evening." With a smooth elegance, he grasped her hand and pressed his lips to her fingers in a lingering caress. Only when she gave a sudden shiver and snatched her hand away to rub it against the satin of her dress did he straighten to smile deep into her eyes. "May I say that you are appearing particularly delectable this evening?"

"What are you doing here?"

Casually leaning against the fluted column, Hart folded his arms across his chest. He discovered it was rather fascinating to watch the play of emotions over her delicate profile. Anger . . . uncertainty . . . and a large dose of unease.

"What any bedazzled fiancé would be doing," he tormented in soft tones. "Basking in the warmth of my beloved's smile. Or at least attempting to bask. You are rather clutch-fisted with your smiles, my love."

Not surprisingly, it was a scowl not a smile that his bride-to-be offered. "If you think to make a scene, Hart . . ."

"A scene?" he interrupted with a lift of his brows. "I am not the one raising my voice like a common fishwife."

Clamping her lips together, Molly shot a covert glance toward the passing crowd. The guests were indeed ogling them, but Hart suspected that for the next several weeks the two of them would not be able to leave their homes without being gawked upon as if they were circus performers. Their mysterious engagement was bound to provoke rabid curiosity of the *ton*. Especially when they managed to behave as two lunatics rather than sensible, somber-minded citizens.

"What do you want, my lord?"

He leaned forward until he could fill himself with the warm scent of lavender. Then, unable to resist temptation, he reached out to stroke his hand along the length of her stubborn jaw.

"I have warned you that is a dangerous question. Even more so when you are attired in a gown that arouses a gentleman's deepest fantasies."

Even above the din of scraping violins and chattering dragons, Hart could hear the sound of her shocked gasp. A satisfied smile touched his lips. Good. It was about damnable time something managed to shock the hoyden.

"Hart?"

Rather distracted by the feel of warm silk beneath his fingers, Hart reluctantly met her wary gaze.

"Yes?"

"I . . . halt that at once," she hissed, although her voice was far from steady.

His lips twitched as his fingers swept down her throat to halt at the wildly fluttering pulse at the base of her neck. Silk and lavender. A most potent force.

"Halt what?" he murmured.

"Touching me as if I am one of your tarts."

A sudden laugh was wrenched from his throat. He had never possessed a tart that managed to anger and arouse him at the same moment. Nor one that haunted his thoughts with such tenacity.

His eyes darkened as he swept his glance over her stiffly held body. "If you were one of my tarts then we would not be standing amongst this dull crowd. And we most certainly would not be wearing so many damnable clothes." He deliberately leaned closer. "Why do we not slip into a quiet room so that I can properly demonstrate?"

Blushing deeply, she abruptly stepped from his hovering proximity. "Certainly not."

"Why so adamant?"

"In the event it has escaped your notice, I am not one of your concubines."

Leaning back against the column, Hart regarded her pinched expression. Despite her attempts to appear condemning, he did not miss the nervous fashion that her hands plucked at her skirts. Nor the uncertainty that darkened her eyes.

Oddly, he discovered he had to battle a renegade flare of tenderness at her seemingly flustered innocence.

"Ah, but you are my fiancée, which implies an even greater intimacy," he pointed out softly. "Soon enough we shall be as close as a man and woman can possibly be. You shall be mine." His gaze swept over her. "Completely and utterly, my love."

"I . . ." She touched her tongue to her lips as she regarded him warily.

"Yes, sweet Molly?"

With an obvious effort, she stiffened her spine and took a firm step backward. "How did you know that I would be here this evening?"

It was not at all what Hart had expected.

THE WEDDING CLAUSE 85

God's teeth. She was supposed to be baffled and frightened. Fluttery. Weak in the knees. Certainly not sharp-witted and suspicious.

He discovered himself abruptly cudgeling his mind for a suitable response. One that did not include the truth.

"There are not so many entertainments at this time of year to make it difficult to deduce which you would choose."

She frowned at his smooth response. "I do not believe you."

"No?"

"No."

"Then perhaps I am a mystic."

She met his gaze squarely. "It is more likely you are having me spied upon."

Hart gave a choked cough. Egads, could the blasted woman never respond as she was supposed to?

"What a suspicious imagination you possess," he managed to murmur in mocking tones. "Do you think I skulk about Lady Falker's townhouse awaiting you to make an appearance?"

"I do not yet know how you manage to follow me, but be assured that I shall discover your methods."

The realization that she was quite clever enough to ferret out the treacherous maid if she put her mind to it, Hart was swift to attempt to distract her.

"What does it matter? Soon enough you will be my wife and not only will you be obliged to tell me of your schedule for every day, but I shall have to offer my approval."

Not surprisingly, she stiffened in obvious revulsion. She was certainly not a woman who would take well to a tight leash. She had been allowed to run willy-nilly for far too long.

"Approval?"

He offered a rather smug smile. "Most certainly. And I must warn you that during the first few months of our marriage I intend to keep you far too occupied to even consider entertainments. Indeed, I think we might retire to my hunting lodge to ensure our privacy. It will be the perfect setting to indulge our cozy explorations of one another."

The beautiful countenance seemed to pale for just a moment before a rush of color stained her cheeks a delicate rose.

"I suppose you hope to frighten me with such talk?" she hissed between clenched teeth.

Hart's lips twisted in rueful humor. Of course he hoped to frighten her. Unfortunately, he was discovering it remarkably tempting to imagine having her at his isolated lodge. Alone with this angel he possessed the premonition that he could easily forget that she was a cold-blooded fortune hunter and simply indulge in the attraction that he had battled since she had burst into his life.

Abruptly shoving from the column, Hart scrubbed away his unwelcome thoughts.

"Frighten? Why should you be frightened?" he demanded softly. "I would rather hope you were filled with delight . . . anticipation . . ."

"Fah."

"I beg your pardon?"

Her features hardened with suspicion. "We both know that you have no intention of wedding me."

Hart shrugged. "Certainly you are not my first choice. Or even last choice, for that matter. But as you have pointed out on more than one occasion this marriage was my grandmother's last request. I must now console myself with the one benefit of being tied to you for all eternity." He paused, allowing his gaze to dip to the satin softness of her lips. "And it is a benefit I intend to enjoy to the fullest, my sweet."

"Hart, this is . . ."

"Ah, Molly. Here you are." Abruptly appearing at Molly's side, Lady Falker regarded Hart with a belligerent expression before turning toward her friend. "I fear that I have developed a shocking headache. I hope you do not mind if we leave now?"

Molly did not even make an attempt to hide her relief. "Of course not. We shall go this moment." Grudgingly, she turned to sweep Hart a shallow curtsey. "I hope you will excuse us, my lord?"

"If I must." Reaching out he took her hand to lift it to his lips, glancing into her dark eyes. "I will call on you tomorrow and we will go for a drive in the park."

"Actually . . . I . . ."

"Yes, my dear?

Longing to damn him to the netherworld, Molly was instead forced to curve her stiff lips into a semblance of a smile. She was, after all, determined to convince him that she intended to be his bride.

"That would be lovely."

Hart smothered a chuckle at her jaundiced expression. Ah yes, soon enough he would have Miss Molly Conwell put properly into her place.

And then he could have her out of his thoughts, and out of his dreams.

Just as it should be.

Chapter Six

Molly had considered a dozen different excuses to avoid meeting with Hart. Every maiden was taught from the cradle the subtle, polite means of evading the more troublesome encroachers and less desirables that one was bound to encounter in society.

Unfortunately, her training had never included how precisely a maiden was suppose to elude her own fiancé.

No doubt a grave oversight of etiquette on the part of her governess.

There surely must be some ghastly illness she could conjure? One that was suitably contagious and able to terrify off the most determined gentleman? A sudden rash or a few boils? Perhaps a convenient brain fever?

In the end, she had come to the unwelcome conclusion that Hart would never be fooled. Even if she were upon her deathbed, he would presume it were some devious attempt to elude him. No, she could not reasonably put off her fiancé. Not without revealing that she was simply playing a desperate game of bluff.

With a sense of foreboding, she allowed herself to be attired in a pretty buttercup gown that possessed a matching cape lined with fur. She complimented it with her sturdiest half boots and a bonnet with a high rim. She might be forced into riding with Hart, but she would be damned if she were going to freeze to death in the process, she told herself.

At last as prepared as she was ever going to be, Molly left the welcome security of her chambers and made her way down to the front parlor. Once again she was struck by a sudden wave of unease. Not particularly surprising, she ruefully acknowledged. Not after last evening.

She was accustomed to Hart's contemptuous disdain. Heaven knew she had endured enough of it over the past year. But last evening, he had not been at all contemptuous. Instead he had been seductive and charming and utterly male. A potent combination that was bound to make any maiden go weak in the knees. Even a maiden who logically knew that his attentions were no more than a deliberate effort to frighten her into flight.

Nervously, she paced from one end of the elegant room to the other, relieved when at last the butler appeared at the door. Surely any confrontation with Hart could not be worse than this constant fretting and stewing?

"Lord Woodhart has arrived, miss."

"Thank you." Smoothing her sweaty palms upon the heavy cape, she offered what she hoped was a confident smile. "Please tell his lordship I will join him in just a few moments."

The butler offered a stiff bow. "Very good."

Waiting until she was once again alone Molly sternly squared her shoulders. Hart was only playing a game. He could not rattle her unless she allowed him to do so.

Repeating the words over and over, she slowly made her way from the large parlor and down the stairs to the black and white foyer. She even managed not to stumble when she caught sight of the large, impressively male form standing next to the door.

Not that it was an easy task, she acknowledged as her breath threatened to lodge in her throat. Especially not when that dark, disturbing gaze moved with a slow, lazy scrutiny over her pale countenance and his lips curved into a tantalizing smile that had to be designed to halt a female heart.

She bit her lip as she forced herself forward. It appeared that he was once again prepared to play the role of the devoted suitor. A knowledge that only tightened the nerves knotted in the pit of her stomach.

As an enemy he was dangerous enough. As a seducer . . . well, it simply did not bear contemplating.

"My angel," he murmured with a faint bow. "As stunning as always."

Ignoring the stupid flutters of her heart, Molly briskly pulled on her soft leather gloves. "Thank you, Hart."

A wicked humor glinted in the dark eyes as if he were perfectly aware of the reaction she refused to reveal.

"Are you prepared?"

"Most certainly."

"Good." With a nod toward the waiting butler,

Hart gently grasped her arm and led her through the door that was promptly pulled open. In silence they moved down the steps, but as they neared the graceful Tilbury he suddenly glanced down with a mysterious smile. "I hope you do not mind, I have brought along a companion."

"A companion?" Allowing herself to be lifted onto the padded bench, Molly frowned until she at last caught sight of the small monkey who was cowering upon the floorboards. Her sharp unease was forgotten as she noted the elegant velvet coat that had been tailored to fit the furry body. "Oh . . . how adorable."

Swinging onto the carriage, Hart took the reins from the waiting groom, and then astonishingly he gave a low whistle that brought the monkey scurrying from his hiding place to climb happily upon his lap.

"I presume that you recall this little scamp?" he murmured as he urged the fiercely large bays into motion.

"Of course." She watched in bemusement as the monkey clung to Hart's arm, clearly quite devoted to his master. "I cannot believe that you kept him."

He flashed her an unreadable glance. "Would you have me toss him in the gutter?"

"Certainly not. I merely assumed that you would have him returned to me."

"No doubt a far wiser choice considering he keeps my household in continuous chaos," he retorted dryly. "Unfortunately Brummel would be devastated to be separated from me, would you not, old chap?"

"Brummel?"

"Well, he is such a dapper scamp, it only seemed fitting."

She was unable to halt the genuine smile that curved her lips. Who the devil would have ever thought that the Heartless Viscount would harbor a weakness for small, fuzzy animals?

"I do not believe Mr. Brummel would discover it quite so fitting," she pointed out.

His lips twitched as he turned onto the busy London thoroughfare. "In his current state of disgrace, I do not fear his wrath. Besides which, Beau has always possessed a rather surprising sense of humor beneath his air of disdain."

"You are friends?"

"Of a sorts," he confirmed in offhand tones.

Molly rolled her eyes as she settled more comfortably. Of course this gentleman was intimately acquainted with Brummel. He was no doubt bosom buddies with the Prince. Men of power and influence would always flock together.

"Somehow I am not at all surprised," she muttered lowly.

He gave a lift of his brows at the edge in her voice. "You possess a dislike of poor Beau even after all the indignities he has suffered?"

"I can hardly dislike someone I have never even encountered, my lord," she retorted. "Mr. Brummel is hardly the sort to take an interest in a mere companion."

Oddly, his lips twisted with amusement at her tart reprimand. "Only because you did not cross his path. Had he suspected that my grandmother harbored a golden-haired angel with eyes the exotic darkness of a tropical night and the lips of a temptress he would have been camped upon her doorstep. If nothing else, he always possessed exquisite taste."

Molly smothered the most ridiculous urge to blush. The gentleman was a master of seduction, she sternly reminded herself. Of course he knew precisely what to say to make a maiden feel all warm and giddy.

"Very pretty, Hart. But of course, I suppose a glib tongue is essential for all successful rakes?"

Expecting him to be angered by her mocking retort, Molly was caught off guard when he merely chuckled with seeming enjoyment.

"I do believe we have just been insulted, Brummel. Surely there must be a penalty for such impertinence?" he demanded of his tiny companion. "What is that? Ah." He slowly smiled as he caught Molly's reluctantly amused gaze. "Brummel insists that you must forfeit a kiss."

Her heart missed a strategic beat as she struggled to appear indifferent to his bold flirtation. A task made all the more difficult by the distinctly odd desire to glance at the chiseled male lips that no doubt knew all there was to know of kisses.

"Indeed?"

"Well, it is only justice."

She primly folded her hands in her lap. "You may inform Brummel that I do not offer kisses to ill-mannered beasts."

"I was not referring to the monkey," he informed her softly.

"Neither was I."

His laughter rang through the chilled air as he efficiently turned his team through the gate to the park. Just for a moment, Molly discovered her gaze lingering upon the elegant profile. He was always astonishingly handsome, even when he was glaring and stomping about. But with his features softened and a pair of unexpected dimples dancing next to his full lips, he was heart stopping.

Abruptly, she turned her head to watch the handful of carriages that threaded through the various lanes. Very well. He was handsome. Achingly handsome. And undoubtedly charming when he desired to make the effort.

That was no excuse to become a babbling idiot.

"Ah, my dear, a direct hit," he was murmuring as they bowled along the nearly empty path. "But while I am wounded, I will not be forgetting that I am due a kiss."

She reluctantly turned back to meet his devilish gaze. It was that or reveal her simmering unease.

"Is demanding forfeits your only means of acquiring kisses, my lord?"

He regarded her with the blithe confidence of a gentleman who knew quite well that his kisses were sought after by every female who was not yet six feet under.

"Only when necessary, my love. As a rule my fatal charm is quite sufficient."

"I have often considered you fatal, but never, I fear, charming."

If anything his expression only became more smug. "That is only because I have never made the attempt in your presence."

Her stomach quivered in sudden warning. "And now you intend to?"

Slowing the high-spirited team, he allowed his gaze to openly roam over her stiff form. Roam and linger, she realized as she unwittingly tugged the cape closer about her.

"What I intend is for the two of us to become better acquainted," he at last clarified.

"Why?"

"I should think that was obvious. Christmas shall soon be upon us and while you may not quibble at wedding a near stranger, I assure you I do. A husband should know something of his wife, even if it is only her favorite color or whether she prefers the left or the right side of the bed."

Wedding. Husband. Hart. Bed.

Her brain temporarily threatened to freeze before she was sucking in a deep breath.

No. This was just a trick. Just another means of attempting to steal away her inheritance. Hell would freeze over before he would take her as a bride.

"A stranger?" She smiled wryly. "I thought you had already concluded you know all there is to know of me. I am, after all, no more than a heartless fortune hunter who swindles old ladies and steals their money."

His countenance hardened at her direct thrust, but with barely a blink he had managed to smooth his features and even summoned a faint smile.

"Since we are doomed to be wed, I must now hope that there is more than simple greed within that distant heart," he murmured.

"Doomed?"

He gave a lift of his shoulder. "An appropriate word for our dilemma would you not say?"

"Not at all." She met his gaze steadily. "Marriage is not inevitable. We both have a choice."

His smile thinned. "A choice we have both seemingly made. Unless you have changed your mind?"

"Certainly not."

"Then it appears we are trapped with each other. Would it not be preferable to be somewhat familiar before we say our vows?"

What could she say to that? To insist that she would far prefer to remain antagonistic enemies would be ludicrous.

"If you wish," she grudgingly conceded.

"Good."

With an unexpected motion, Hart pulled the bays to a slow halt. Then, with an elegant flare he tossed the reins to the groom who had promptly leapt to the paved avenue.

Molly regarded him with a surge of wariness. "What are you doing?"

"I thought you might enjoy a stroll. It is difficult to concentrate while controlling these brutes." His smile dared her to refuse. "Now . . . shall we become better acquainted?"

Well, matters were progressing just dashingly, Hart assured himself.

Despite Molly's seemingly calm demeanor as he handed her down from the carriage and led her along the remote lane of the park, he could not miss the faint shiver that raced through her body.

The fact that he could not completely control his own shivers of awareness as her hand lightly clutched his arm was a complication he stubbornly attempted to dismiss.

Of course he shivered. And tingled. And tugged her closer than was strictly necessary.

He had already accepted the unpalatable truth. She was a woman, and most certainly he was a man. A very virile man. It was inevitable that such close proximity was bound to stir and rouse sensations.

Sucking in a deep breath gently spiced with lavender, Hart determinedly girded himself for battle. And that was what this was, he sternly reminded himself. Not seduction, but war.

"Are you cold?" he murmured.

"The wind is rather cutting," she admitted.

"Here." With an elegant flourish, Hart removed his heavy caped coat and gently draped it about her slender form. "This should keep you warm."

She briefly stumbled, as if caught off guard by his thoughtful gesture, her head abruptly lifting to meet his searching gaze.

"But you will freeze."

"I shall survive." He deliberately smiled deep into her eyes. "Besides which, as your fiancé it is my pleasure to ensure your comfort."

Her breath seemed to catch before she was determinedly forcing a smile to her lips. "Good heavens, Hart, you might almost convince me you are a gentleman."

"Oh, I should never desire to attain such a tedious title."

"You prefer being a dangerous rake?"

His soft chuckle echoed through the near silence that surrounded them. "I prefer living by my own rules, not those dictated by blithering idiots."

Unexpectedly, her eyes darkened at his teasing words. Almost as if he had somehow distressed her.

"A fortunate thing that you are wealthy and titled and in the position to flaunt society. Not all of us are so lucky."

Hart frowned at her peculiar reaction. "Do I detect a trace of bitterness, sweet Molly? Do you secretly long to dare convention and damn the consequences?"

"Actually, I fear I am quite conventional." A rather wistful smile curved her lips. "I have never sought nor desired anything more than a peaceful existence in the country with a family to call my own. Rather boring, I know, but it seems like paradise to me."

A disturbing urge to pull her close and assure her that her dream was not at all boring, but instead remarkably similar to one that he had harbored until Victoria had taught him such a bitter lesson in trust, was sternly squashed. Miss Molly Conwell would claim that she loved puppies, small children and butterflies if she thought it would undermine his suspicions.

"You must forgive me if I discover that difficult to believe," he murmured.

Her expression hardened. "Why?"

"Because I have already offered you an ample sum to live quite peacefully in the country," he pointed out. "If you only wished a tidy cottage and life of bucolic pleasure, you would have leaped at such an opportunity."

"I . . ." She abruptly lowered her gaze as if wary of revealing her inner thoughts. "I cannot put aside your grandmother's request so easily."

The lie was obvious, but the stab of disappointment that shot through his heart at her deception was unforeseen. And entirely unwelcome.

"Of course not," he muttered.

She stiffened at the edge in his voice. "She was very good to me."

"Oh yes, thirty thousand pounds good to you."

Her head ducked even lower. "Yes."

Just for a moment, his gaze lingered upon the vulnerable curve of her exposed nape. Ridiculously, his fingers curled at his side. He was uncertain if he itched to test the softness of the pale skin or throttle her.

Perhaps both.

"You do realize that as my wife you will have to spend most of your time in London?" he abruptly demanded. "Parliament, as well as my business, keeps me here much of the year."

There was a heavy silence before she was lifting her head to meet his glittering gaze with a tight smile.

"I thought I was to be banished to your hunting lodge?"

Hart sucked in a sharp breath as he came to a slow halt. Through the long, sleepless night he had been plagued with images of his hunting lodge and the damnable pleasure of having this woman at his mercy. Now he could no more halt his sudden stirring of desire than he could have halted the chilled wind.

And why should he? Wasn't his scheme to convince her that he desired her enough to offer her marriage?

"Ah yes, the hunting lodge." His hands lifted to grasp her shoulders so that he could turn her to face him. "You should not remind me of such a delectable fantasy. Not until after we are safely wed."

"I did not mean . . ." Her words trailed away as he slowly, but steadily began to pull her toward him. "Hart."

"Yes?"

"You must let me go. Someone will see us."

"And what if they do?" he murmured softly. "Surely engaged couples are expected to indulge in an occasional kiss?"

Her eyes widened in shock. "Not in the midst of the park."

"It is somewhat public for my taste." He offered a lift of his shoulder, even as a wicked glimmer of determination smoldered to life in his eyes. "Still, beggars as they say cannot be choosers."

"Oh."

His gaze dropped to the lush temptation of her lips. Within his mind, he was calculating precisely what sort of kiss he should offer. Stark and passionate, he concluded. Something designed to send a virgin into fluttering panic. At the same moment his head was lowering to cover her mouth with his own and any sensible thought was lost in a cloud of lavender pleasure.

There was no pouncing, no strategic effort to

terrify her with lust. Instead his lips softened and with a tender care he cupped her face in his hands, tasting of her innocence with a slow thoroughness that made his heart pound. Dear lord. She tasted as he dreamed spring would taste. Pure and fresh and sweet as honey.

For endless moments he savored the velvet heat. A savoring that might have continued indefinitely if Molly had not suddenly stiffened and arched her back in his arms.

"Hart. Someone is approaching."

Silently cursing the decidedly untimely intrusion, Hart lowered his arms and turned to glare at the nearby bushes that were rattling in an odd manner. For a moment, he presumed that it must have been a squirrel or stray dog that had startled Molly. Then with a sudden flurry a small, decidedly angry monkey scurried through the thick foliage and headed directly for a tall oak tree. Directly behind the beast was an equally angry groom who had considerably more difficulty in battling his way through the bush.

"Good God," he breathed, his brows drawing together at the ridiculous farce. "Harrington, explain yourself."

Red in the face and breathing hard the groom attempted to straighten his uniform. "I am sorry, sir. I turned my head only a moment and the beast bolted."

"May I hope you have not also released my bays to the wild?"

"No, sir, they are properly secured."

"Good. Please see to them while I attempt to rescue Brummel."

Relief at having gotten off so easily rippled over the youthful countenance before the servant was offering a hasty bow.

"Very good, sir."

Without bothering to watch Harrington's rapid retreat, Hart moved toward the towering oak tree and regarded the chattering monkey in exasperation. Although the creature was perched on one of the lower limbs there was no possibility of retrieving him. At least not without an effort.

There was a whiff of lavender before Hart could sense Molly moving to stand beside him.

"Will he come down, do you think?" she demanded.

"The demon from the netherworld?" He flashed her a dry smile. "Not until hell freezes over."

"He looks so frightened."

"That is his stock in trade. He loves nothing more than luring you close with that pathetic expression so that he may toss something upon your head. He lobbed a bowl of custard upon my chef only yesterday."

She turned those melting brown eyes upon him with an expression of concern. "You are not going to leave him up there, are you?"

He briefly found himself lost in those pleading eyes before he was sternly returning his attention to matters at hand. Dash it all. It was one thing to enjoy a woman's kisses. What gentleman wouldn't? It was quite another to moon over her eyes.

"It is no doubt what he deserves, but no, I will not leave him. He adds a bit of amusement to my days. If you would be so good as to hold these."

Removing his hat and gloves, he placed them in her willing hands. Then he began rolling up the sleeves of his linen shirt.

"You will take care?" she muttered.

With a lift of his brows, he flicked a gentle finger over her cheek. "Do not fear, my sweet Molly. I have no intention of missing our wedding night."

"Fah." She stepped away at his light teasing. "I could never be so fortunate."

With a chuckle, Hart turned to make his way toward the towering tree. It took little effort to grasp the lowest branch and swing himself upward. Nor even to inch his way toward Brummel. He had, after all, spent his boyhood years climbing trees, fences and even the occasional building upon his father's estate.

It was not until he had almost reached his unpredictable pet that disaster struck.

Reaching down to retrieve the monkey there was the sharp bark of a dog in the distance. The noise unexpectedly startled the high-strung Brummel and with a shrill cry he launched himself directly at Hart's chest. There was a brief moment when he wavered and nearly caught his balance. But gravity, with its usual perversity, in the end won the battle.

He possessed the sense to clutch the monkey close as he tumbled through the air and to turn so that he landed upon his back rather than his face. Still, the frozen ground refused to give as he hit and the air was roughly jerked from his body.

With a groan, he closed his eyes and mentally judged his various aches and pangs to ensure that nothing was irreparably damaged. He had just concluded that all was relatively well when pair of soft hands were cupping his face and the warmth of Molly's breath was brushing his lips.

"Hart. Oh, God. Are you injured?"

Startled by her frantic tone, Hart wrenched open his eyes to discover her kneeling beside him on the frozen ground. There was no mistaking the concern that tightened her features and darkened her eyes. He shifted uncomfortably, not at all accustomed to having someone fret over him.

"Nothing more than a bruised pride," he muttered, turning his head to glare at the monkey who was currently pulling his hair. "You worthless creature. I should have left you to feed the local vultures."

"You are bleeding," Molly murmured, and then before he could halt her, she had pulled out her handkerchief and was pressing it to the blood seeping through the rip in the knee of his breeches.

His breath caught in his throat. Not from the wound. Or even the blood swiftly soaking her handkerchief. But quite simply from the gentle manner she tended his injury. A gentleness he had not experienced since the death of his mother.

"'Tis nothing, Molly," he said huskily.

She continued to lightly dab his injury with the handkerchief, her expression one of concern. "It is quite deep. You must have hit it upon the limb."

Against his will, Hart discovered his gaze lingering upon the purity of her countenance as she leaned over him. A warmth flared through him.

Not the familiar heat of passion. But a deeper, more disturbing sensation that made him stiffen in sudden alarm.

"You will ruin your gloves," he muttered, shifting away from her soothing touch.

Glancing at him in puzzled surprise, she offered him a faint frown. "They can be replaced. You must have the wound properly cleaned and bandaged."

"Molly, it is just a scratch."

"A scratch that could easily become infected unless given the proper attention."

"I . . ." He gritted his teeth as he battled the urge to reach out and touch her cheek. Surely the fall must have rattled his senses? Or at least his brains. That could be the only excuse for longing to pull her into his arms to simply hold her close.

"Yes?"

Awkwardly holding Brummel in one arm, he scrambled to his feet. He had made fool enough of himself for one day. It was time to retreat before he did something even more absurd.

"We must go."

Chapter Seven

Hart paced from one end of the vaulted library to the other.

He refused to concede that his restless, continuous circuit might have anything to do with his encounter with Miss Molly Conwell the day before.

Why should he?

A man had the right to pace his library if he might want. When he was bored. Or had some trouble upon his mind. Or even when awaiting a visitor. The fact that he had never before paced his library, not even when he had discovered the treacherous truth of Victoria, was not allowed to enter his thoughts.

He desired to pace, and that was precisely what he would do.

Or at least what he desired to do until his butler was ill-mannered enough to thrust open the closed door and announce that a visitor had arrived.

Coming to an abrupt halt, Hart turned to inform the servant that he was not receiving callers only to be outmaneuvered when his cousin bullied his way through the door and offered a sweeping bow.

"Ah, Hart. I hoped to find you at home."

With a rueful wave of his hand toward the startled butler, Hart waited until the door was once again closed before regarding his guest with an expectant expression.

"Thorpe, and at my humble abode, no less. Has the sky fallen or are you simply lost?"

With a shrug, the handsome nobleman tossed aside his high beaver hat and gloves. "This is hardly the first occasion I have called upon you, dear cousin."

"True enough." His lips twitched with suppressed amusement. "There was the occasion when you were foxed and terrorizing the streets of London until the Watch dumped you upon my doorstep. And of course, the charming evening you hid in my cellars after Lord Stanford threatened to castrate you with a dull spoon."

Lifting his quizzing glass, Lord Thorpe peered at Hart in an imperious manner. "Good God, I begin to recall why I do not visit. Surely you do not dredge up the past sins of all your callers, Hart? Otherwise I should think you are a very lonely gentleman."

"Only my favorite cousins," he admitted with a chuckle, moving to a side bar to pour them both a healthy measure of brandy. Returning to Thorpe, he pressed one of the glasses into his cousin's willing hand. "Here."

"I suppose it might help to soothe my wounded sensibilities."

"It usually does."

Thorpe raised his glass in a silent toast before tossing the fiery spirit down in one gulp. "Ah . . . French."

"But of course." Polishing off his own brandy, Hart set aside his glass and crossed his arms over his chest. He was quite certain that Thorpe was not here for a social call. "Now tell me what brings you here, Thorpe, beyond my extraordinary wit and charm."

Strolling casually across the patterned carpet, Thorpe lowered his tall frame onto one of the numerous leather chairs scattered throughout the room and stretched out his legs in a negligent fashion.

"Actually I heard the most amusing tale that I simply had to share with you."

Hart narrowed his gaze, sensing that he was not going to find the tale nearly as amusing as his cousin.

"Indeed?"

"Yes, it seems that a certain Viscount, who shall remain nameless, was noted yesterday lying on his back in the middle of the park with a monkey perched upon his chest and a lovely young maiden making very bold advances upon his leg."

Well, he had been correct. He did not find it nearly so amusing.

Oh, it was not his concern at having made a spectacle of himself in the park. For the past four years, he had refused to trouble himself with what the gossips might have to say. Why would any man of sense be troubled by the innuendoes and half-truths that ran rife through society? Besides which, his position and wealth ensured that he was immune to being ostracized by even the most priggish of hostesses.

No, it was not scandal that troubled him, but

the memory of soft hands tenderly nursing his wound, and velvet brown eyes dark with concern.

His gut twisted even as he attempted to smother the unwelcome memory.

"How peculiar," he at last drawled.

"My thought precisely." Thorpe allowed his lips to curve into a small smile. "One would only expect to view such an exhibition at the theatre. Or that rather naughty brothel next to the docks."

"Very amusing."

"So . . . tell."

Hart managed an annoyingly bland expression. "Tell what?"

Thorpe tapped impatient fingers upon the arm of his chair. "Hart, I am not above giving you a well deserved thrashing if you do not tell me precisely what was occurring in that park."

"You believe that you are capable of thrashing me?"

"I have proven it often enough."

Hart tilted back his head to laugh with sudden enjoyment. This bantering was a familiar balm to his current state of unease.

"I believe the numerous occasions that I beat you senseless has rattled your memory, old chap."

"If it pleases you to think so." Thorpe pretended to smother a yawn before leaning slowly forward with a determined expression. "Now come, Hart. I am not leaving until you have confessed all."

"Do you know, the older I grow the more I realize the benefits of being an orphan?"

"Hart."

Hart heaved a sigh. His damnable cousin was just stubborn enough to perch upon that chair until they both keeled over in old age. Besides which, it was not as if he had anything to hide, did he?

"Oh, very well." Moving toward Thorpe, he took a seat in a matching chair. "Brummel managed to escape from my groom . . ."

"Your groom was holding Brummel hostage?"

"My monkey."

"Monkey? Ah . . . the nasty creature that Miss Conwell sent to the club."

"Yes."

A rather disturbing expression descended upon the lean countenance. "You kept him?"

Hart discovered himself shifting uncomfortably upon the leather. "Do you wish to hear the tale or not?"

"Forgive me." Thorpe offered a wave of his slender hand. "Do please continue."

"As I said, Brummel escaped and being a monkey his first instinct was to climb the largest, most inconvenient tree about."

"Naturally."

"I had little choice but to attempt a rescue."

Thorpe widened his eyes at the clipped words. "Good God, do not tell me that you fell out of the tree?"

The most embarrassing urge to blush was sternly quashed. "Yes."

There was a moment of silence and then without warning, Thorpe doubled over as he laughed with rich amusement at Hart's public mishap. Watching his cousin's merriment with a lift of his brow, Hart waited for him to regain his composure.

After what seemed to be an excessive length

of time, Thorpe at last straightened and wiped his eyes.

"Oh . . . forgive me."

"No, please," Hart drawled. "My wounded dignity was only in need of your unfettered amusement to ensure it is destroyed beyond repair."

The dark eyes twinkled with unrepentant humor. "Even you must admit that a peer of the realm tumbling from a tree clutching a monkey in a satin coat is somewhat humorous."

Reluctantly, Hart leaned back in his seat, his own lips twisting in dry amusement. He supposed that aggravating relative did have a point. Certainly, he would have taken great pleasure in discovering Thorpe in a similarly ridiculous situation.

"If it had been any other peer beyond myself," he grudgingly conceded.

"I only wish I could have been there to witness the spectacle."

"All right, Thorpe, you have had your little jest. Was there anything else?"

Settling back in his seat, Thorpe casually smoothed his dove gray coat and adjusted his cuffs before regarding Hart with a searching gaze.

"As a matter of fact my curiosity was only mildly stirred by your reclining position in the park and the monkey upon your chest," he revealed in low tones. "My true interest is in the female who was openly fondling your leg. Who was she?"

For a moment Hart wavered. It was not that he desired to protect Molly from scandal, he hastily reassured himself. Or to keep her from being harmed by those sharp-tongued harpies who fed upon such gossip. It was just . . .

What?

Abruptly, he squared his shoulders. He was being absurd. They had clearly been seen in the park. Her name was destined to be making the rounds with or without his discretion.

"Miss Conwell."

A dark brow arched. "The mercenary angel?"

"Yes."

"Did she attack you while you were incapacitated?"

"Of course not." He frowned at the ridiculous accusation. "I injured my knee when I fell and like every female she felt the need to flutter over a spot of blood as if I had lost a limb."

"Fluttered, did she?" Thorpe tilted his head to one side. "Rather odd for a harridan who cares for nothing beyond wealth."

The very fact that Thorpe had hit precisely upon what had troubled him for the past hours only deepened his unease. He did not want to think of Molly as tender or caring or vulnerable. Not when he was determined to brand her a thief.

"No doubt she was in shock," he forced himself to mutter. "She must have seen her ill-gained fortune disappearing before her very eyes when I tumbled from the tree."

"Is that what you truly believe?" his cousin prompted.

Hart lifted a hand to rub the tense muscles of his neck. "Bloody hell, I do not know what I believe. The woman is destined to land me in Bedlam."

Thorpe appeared far from comforted by his

reluctant confession. In fact, his features hardened in a manner Hart knew all too well.

"Hart, I think you should take care."

"Do not fear. I have no intention of climbing any more trees in the foreseeable future."

"I was referring to Miss Conwell."

Sensing the lecture that was in the offing, Hart attempted a smile. The last thing he needed was a warning upon handling women by his rakehell of a cousin.

"Miss Conwell? I am hardly in danger from a female who barely reaches my shoulder and who I could crush with one hand."

Thorpe narrowed his gaze at Hart's light tone. "A woman's danger is never her size. Indeed, the more fragile and vulnerable she seems the more lethal she becomes."

Lethal? Hart abruptly rose to his feet, pacing toward the marble chimneypiece. He was immune to coy flirtations, flattery and even practiced seductions. Surely to goodness he could be immune to kindness?

Yes . . . yes, of course he could.

He jutted out his chin in determination. "What are you implying, Thorpe? That I am ridiculous enough to be taken in by a heartless fortune hunter?" he demanded, as much for his benefit as for his cousin.

Thorpe slowly rose. "Not as long you recall that she *is* heartless."

"I am not a fool."

"No, you are a man and, from your own lips, she is a beautiful and desirable woman. A combination that has started wars and brought down empires for centuries."

Hart blinked at the fierce words. It was distinctly out of character for a gentleman who rarely troubled himself over anything.

"Do you not think that you are being somewhat melodramatic?"

Thorpe at least possessed the grace to smile with a wry humor. "Perhaps, but I did gain your attention." Stepping forward, he reached out to grasp Hart's shoulder. "Listen to me—I recall the last occasion you tumbled for pretty blue eyes, and while I thoroughly approve of you discovering a sweet, proper maiden to offer you the necessary heirs, I do not desire to witness you wallowing in black grief once again."

Hart grimaced, well aware he would have never made it through that ghastly betrayal without Thorpe's incessant refusal to leave him to his misery. He surely owed his cousin the assurance that he was not once again to play the fool.

"You have made your point," he said softly.

Thorpe regarded him steadily. "As difficult as it might be to believe, I do care for you, cousin. I want only what is best."

"I know."

"Good." Thorpe abruptly slapped him on the back, nearly toppling Hart onto his face. "Then what do you say to the notion of toddling ourselves off to the club and drinking until we are both too bosky to stand?"

**

After nearly two hours of tossing and turning in her bed, Molly at last gave up all pretense. Blast. It was obvious that she was not about to tumble off to sleep any time soon. In truth, she was accomplishing nothing more than rubbing her skin raw upon the linen sheets. Surely, she would be just as comfortable pacing the floor as continuing her futile bid for rest?

Rising she reached for a light robe to cover her night rail and without bothering with a candle, she slipped through the silent house. She had no particular destination in mind, but somehow her feet carried her through the darkened halls and out the French windows to the back garden.

Perhaps it was the soft scent of roses that called to her, she mused. Or the beauty of the silver-drenched paths. Such things reminded her forcibly of her beloved home. A home that seemed so far away at the moment.

Whatever the reason, she discovered herself drifting farther into the shadows as if she could somehow lose herself in the dark peace that surrounded her.

A hopeless task, she slowly discovered. With a grimace, she at last paused beside the ivy covered gate that led to the mews. Even alone in the isolated garden, she could feel an odd tension clenching her stomach and a tingle of awareness steal across her skin. She could even smell the tantalizing scent of male cologne.

Damn, Hart.

How could he cause her such unease when he wasn't even near?

Or at least he shouldn't be near.

Once again catching a distinct whiff of familiar cologne, Molly stiffened as the gate was slowly pressed open and a large, male form stepped into the garden.

Her eyes widened as she took a hasty step backward. "Good God . . . Hart."

Leaving the gate open, Hart briefly paused before he moved toward her, his gait less than steady. Not until he was standing far too close did he come to a halt.

"You should not be out here," he muttered, his voice oddly thick as he reached out to touch one of her golden curls.

"What?"

"It is very late, and all know that the night is the time for sinners. Angels should be safely tucked in their beds."

Pressing a hand to her racing heart, Molly allowed her gaze to sweep over the unexpected intruder. It was undoubtedly Hart. There was no mistaking the fiercely handsome countenance and muscular body. No other gentleman could claim such perfection.

Still, there was something . . . different about him.

It was in the manner his hair was tousled to tumble onto his wide brow and the undoubted hint of dishabille of his elegant clothes. There was an untamed rakishness about him that made a shiver of warning inch down her spine.

"What are you doing here, Hart?" she demanded in suspicious tones.

"The truth?"

"Of course."

"I do not know." A self-derisive smile curled the corners of his mouth. "I should be with Thorpe enjoying a night of revelry. That was my plans, after all. But it did not seem to matter how much wine I consumed, or how many hands of cards I might win, I could not keep myself away." His fingers drifted to her pale cheek. "Perhaps you are not an angel at all, but rather a siren that calls to me."

Her breath quickened at the dark, husky tones. Oh heavens. She had thought his smooth seduction skills were dangerous. But tonight he was not the practiced rake. He was pure male predator.

"I think perhaps you are a bit foxed," she retorted.

"More than a bit," he agreed.

"You should go to your home."

His smile twisted as his fingers softly brushed her lips. "Home? What home?"

She frowned. "You do not recall where you reside?"

"Oh, I recall that I have grand estates and elegant townhouses and even magnificent hunting lodges that strike envy in the hearts of my friends. And I could no doubt locate them blindfolded if need be. But what home do I have?"

Molly stilled as she regarded the countenance that appeared unexpectedly vulnerable in the soft silver light.

"What do you mean?"

"I mean that you were right," he husked. "I have no one. No close family. No one I truly trust. And there are times when I rattle about in those vast houses and feel as if I am a stranger there."

Unwelcome tenderness rushed through Molly

at his unwitting confession. Blast it all. She did not want to feel sorry for this gentleman. Not when she was so very close to saving her brother from his horrid fate.

"Hart, you are not at all yourself this evening," she murmured softly. "I think it best you leave."

He did not even seem to hear her words as his gaze drifted over her upturned countenance. "What of you, Molly? Do you have some place to call home? Some place where you know you belong?"

Her breath caught as her heart twisted with a sudden ache of loss. "I did."

"But not now?"

"No." She swallowed heavily. "Not now."

"A lost angel, is that what you are, Molly?" he whispered in distracted tones, his thoughts seemingly consumed by the manner his fingers continued to caress her lips. "Or are you a temptress sent to deceive and torment?"

Deceive and torment? Her? He was the one sneaking into private gardens and making her shiver with his warm touch. He was the one who made sleep impossible and plagued her with thoughts better left unthought.

Botheration. He was an utter devil.

"Hart, it is very late," she managed to rasp, unnerved by the sensation of her lips brushing his gentle fingertips.

"And yet here you are, roaming through the darkness," he murmured. "Tell me why, angel. What haunts your dreams?"

"Nothing."

He offered a click of his tongue. "Oh no. You

would be nicely tucked in your bed if something did not trouble you. Innocents are allowed to sleep the sleep of the just. It is the wicked who seek the night."

He struck far too close to the truth and Molly stiffened with a flare of guilt. "If that is true then you must be wicked as well."

"But, of course." His lips twitched. "I have never claimed to be a saint."

"A wise choice since no one would ever believe it of you."

"No doubt. Still, it has never bothered me. Being a saint must be a tedious business." His gaze drifted over her countenance, lingering a long moment upon her lips. "'Tis far more pleasant to seduce beautiful maidens in the garden."

"Indeed? And I suppose you have seduced any number in the garden?" she demanded in tones far more sharp than she had intended.

Expecting a flippant retort Molly was caught off guard when his features seemed to become gaunt in the silver shadows. As if he were harried beyond bearing.

"Not for longer than I care to admit," he muttered. "I have not even thought of another woman. Not since I have been plagued and haunted by a lavender-scented angel. God, but you torment me."

A swift, perilous heat rushed through Molly as his eyes darkened with unmistakable intent. Oh lord. He was going to kiss her. And worse, she could already feel her body swaying toward his welcome heat.

"Hart, you should not be here," she forced herself to say. "You must leave."

The male fingers abruptly shifted to cup her chin and lift her countenance to his smoldering gaze. "Is that what you want, Molly? To be alone in the moonlight?"

No, it wasn't what she wanted, blast it all. She had been alone for so terribly long. And to be held in warm, strong arms for even a few moments was a temptation that was making her ache.

"Hart . . . please. Go."

He sucked in a deep breath as his head lowered until his forehead rested against her own. "Very well. I will go, but we both know that I will return." He gave a low rasping laugh. "I cannot seem to help myself. Until then . . ." His lips trailed sweetly over her cheek. "Sleep well, my angel."

Chapter Eight

"I do not like this, Molly." Clasping her hands together Georgie paced back and forth through the back parlor. With every turn, she deliberately glanced at the silent Molly seated upon a brocade sofa as if to ensure that her stern lecture was not falling upon deaf ears. "It was horrid enough when Lord Woodhart was stomping about and breathing threats. But for him to now insist that he is prepared to go through with the wedding . . . well, it simply does not bear contemplating."

Molly heaved an inward sigh. Why had she not simply stayed in her chambers as she had been wont to do? Goodness knew that after yet another sleepless night plagued by thoughts of a tall, deliciously dark gentleman she could have used the rest. And as an unexpected windfall, she could have entirely missed this unwelcome sermon upon the dangers of her chosen path.

Unfortunately, she knew Georgie all too well. If she sensed even a hint that Molly was attempting to avoid her, she would have harangued and bothered her until she knew every sordid detail. And the last thing she wanted was her friend discovering that Hart had been skulking in the gardens last night.

Gads, she was nearly livid at the mere thought that Molly had taken an innocuous carriage ride with the man. If she knew that Molly had met him in the dark without a chaperone in sight, there was no telling what she would do.

Her heart gave a renegade flutter before she ruthlessly squelched her absurd reaction. No. She would not dwell upon memories better left forgotten. Last night Hart had been cast to the wind. And like any sodden male he had babbled a lot of nonsense. Only a mooncalf would think being called an angel and nearly kissed in the moonlight by a foxed nobleman as thrilling.

That was even if it hadn't all been a part of his ruthless scheme in the first place.

Squaring her shoulders, she returned her attention to the woman currently regarding her with an anxious frown.

"Lord Woodhart has no intention of ever wedding me, Georgie," she said in patient tones. "This is nothing more than his latest ploy to frighten me."

Dark brows arched in disbelief. "And how can you be so certain?"

Molly smiled wryly. "Do you honestly believe he would tie himself to a scheming fortune hunter?"

"If it keeps you from his inheritance."

"Nonsense." Molly gave a humorless laugh. "He is far too proud to tarnish his name with a penniless maiden who has been forced to labor as a mere servant. Besides which, I do not doubt when Hart does finally wed it will be to a timid, biddable creature he can keep firmly upon his leash."

Georgie gave a slow shake of her head. "You are presuming a great deal, Molly. What if you are mistaken?"

Molly stubbornly jutted out her chin. Georgie was becoming as ridiculous as Andrew. How could either one possibly imagine that Hart would ever lower himself to taking a wife that would be no more than an embarrassment to him? It was absurd.

Almost as absurd as the ill-mannered pang that flared through her heart.

"I am not mistaken," she retorted in disgruntled tones.

"And if you are not?"

Molly heaved an exasperated sigh. Gads, what did she have to do? Put Hart on the rack so that he would admit he would rather be . . . what had he said . . . drawn and quartered before taking her as his bride?

"Please, Georgie, let us not argue," she pleaded.

Georgie's expression swiftly softened. "Forgive me, Molly, but I cannot help but be concerned. You can be very naive in regards to gentlemen."

"Fah, you have no need to remind me. No one knows better than I that I have never even had a suitor. Still, having a brother has given me some insight. I know that gentlemen enjoy tossing about orders and making a show of their masculine pride. I also know that they will do anything to protect their family and their reputation." Molly's expression unwittingly hardened with a hint of bitterness. "Hart would not wed me even if he did not believe I was a money grubbing tart."

Georgie slowly wrapped her arms about her waist as she regarded Molly with an arrested frown.

"Molly."

"What?"

"You . . ."

Molly lifted her brows at her friend's odd manner. "What?"

"Lord Woodhart has not . . . turned your head, has he?"

"Turned my head?"

"Are you infatuated with the man?"

A surge of crimson heat stained Molly's cheeks even as she abruptly rose to her feet. "Why ever would you say such a thing? You must know that I detest Lord Woodhart."

"I also know he is charming, handsome and overly blessed with the sort of male allure that make the most sensible female a bit noddy."

As improbable as it might be, Molly felt her cheeks flame even hotter. Botheration. Yes, Hart was charming and obnoxiously handsome and oozing with allure. And there were moments last night when he gazed at her with such a haunted need that it made her heart leap. But . . . infatuated?

That was impossible.

Was it not?

"Georgie," she muttered in protest.

"Do you deny you are developing feelings for Lord Woodhart?"

"I do not even like Hart."

A rather grim smile touched Georgie's lips. "Liking and wanting have nothing to do with one another. On this subject I know all too well."

Molly blinked in surprise at the strange words, but even as she opened her mouth to question her friend more closely the door to the parlor was thrust wide and a chamber maid entered the room with a small curtsey.

"Beg pardon, my lady."

With obvious reluctance, Georgie turned to regard the servant with a hint of impatience. Clearly, her lecture was far from over.

"What is it, Daisy?"

Holding out her arms the maid revealed a long box tied with pretty yellow ribbon. "A package has been delivered for Miss Conwell."

Molly gave a start of surprise. "For me?"

"Yes, miss."

With an unexplainable wariness Molly moved to take the package from the waiting servant. "Thank you."

"Who ever is it from?" Georgie demanded as Molly crossed to lay the package upon the sofa and struggled with the ribbon.

"I haven't the faintest notion."

"There is no note?"

"No, I . . ." Having at last pulled the bow free Molly tipped off the lid of the box and felt the breath being squeezed from her body. "Oh."

With a rustle of silk, Georgie was peering over Molly's shoulder and giving a shocked sigh of pleasure at the dozens of elegant gloves that had been revealed. And no wonder, Molly acknowledged in dazed puzzlement, her fingers reaching to lightly touch a pair of ivory kidskin gloves.

"Good heavens, they are exquisite," Georgie murmured.

"Yes, they are."

"Who could have sent them? Andrew?"

An unknowingly secretive smile touched Molly's mouth as realization bloomed within her. "Hart."

"Lord Woodhart?" Without warning, Georgie was moving to stand before her, an expression of disapproval marring her pretty features. "Molly, I want the truth from you."

Startled by the sudden attack, Molly could only shake her head in bewilderment. "The truth about what?"

"Why would he send you such a lavish gift if he is determined to be rid of you?"

Molly shifted uneasily. "I ruined my gloves while tending to his wound. This is no doubt his absurd means of revealing his appreciation."

Even to her own ears the explanation sounded lame, and it was no surprise when Georgie planted her hands upon her hips in obvious disbelief.

"Indeed?"

"For goodness sake." Molly hastily moved to return the lid to the box and gathered it into her arms. "'Tis nothing to make such a fuss about."

"Then why are you flushed?"

"Perhaps because you have been fussing over me like a mother hen," she retorted in exasperation. "There is nothing to concern you in regards to Lord Woodhart. I assure you that all will be well."

Georgie's features only hardened in determination. "I intend to make very sure that it is."

Feeling oddly vulnerable and not at all inclined to be badgered further, Molly clutched the box tighter to her chest. "If you will forgive me, Georgie, I believe I shall lay down for a bit."

Not waiting for a response, Molly swept from the parlor. Blast Hart. Someday soon she would stop allowing him to unnerve her with such ease.

Someday very, very soon.

Hart waited nearly a week before once again searching out Molly.

He assured himself that he was merely allowing the vixen to stew and brood upon the dangers of her present course. It was, after all, a sound ploy. Every military man knew that to attack and then retreat without warning often undermined the courage of the opponent.

Unfortunately, an evil voice continued to whisper in the back of his mind that his reluctance to seek out Molly had nothing to do with military strategy. Instead it had every thing to do with his stunningly ridiculous behavior in her moon-drenched garden.

Even days later he cringed at the memory of his brandy sodden behavior. He had been an utter fool to give into his impulse to linger outside Molly's window as if he were some sort of moonstruck schoolboy. And an even bigger fool not to flee the moment she had entered the shadowed garden.

But with his blood heated by strong spirits and a

THE WEDDING CLAUSE   129

clamoring ache to taste of her lips once again clouding his mind, he had been unable to walk away. He had to be near her no matter what the danger.

It was not until this morning that he had at last arisen with a newfound determination. Christmas was creeping ever closer and he was still not rid of his unwelcome fiancée. It was time to remind himself of precisely why he could not allow Molly to arrive at that chapel.

And he knew the perfect means of doing so.

Attiring himself with care in a black coat matched with dove gray breeches and silver waistcoat, he called for his Tilbury and headed for Lady Falker's townhouse. It was far too early for a social call, but conveniently when he pulled onto the elegant cul-de-sac he discovered Molly just entering the street.

With a tidy flourish Hart tugged his anxious grays to a halt and gave a tip of his beaver hat.

"Ah, excellent timing, my dear," he murmured, refusing to allow his gaze to dwell upon the precise manner the ivory spenser hugged her slender form or how the chilled breeze tugged the jade skirts to reveal an enticing curve of her leg.

Stiffening at his abrupt appearance the delicate angel offered a grudging curtsey rather than bolting as she so obviously desired to do.

"Good morning, my lord."

"Please, Molly, no 'my lords' so early in the day," he protested.

Rising, she forced herself to meet his amused gaze with a cool composure. Only the hint of color upon her cheeks revealed her inner apprehension. An apprehension that should have pleased Hart but instead made his chest tighten with an unexplainable regret.

"Have you come to call?"

Giving himself a mental shake, Hart hardened his resolve. He was here with one purpose and one purpose only. And that was to prove to himself once and for all that Molly Conwell was nothing more than a fortune hunting tart.

"Actually I have come to collect you," he informed her in clipped tones.

"Collect me?"

"You did mention the need to acquire a trousseau," he reminded her. "We had best begin the fittings if you wish it completed before the wedding."

She frowned in confusion. "You wish to accompany me shopping?"

"Well, you are not yet familiar with my preferences. How can you hope to please me if I do not help you choose your gowns?"

The stiffness threatened to settle permanently in the slender body as she offered him a frozen glare. "It appears you have wasted a trip across town, my lord. I choose my gowns to please myself, no one else."

He lazily lifted his brows. "At least I should be allowed to select your night attire? There at least you will wish to please me. I possess a decided weakness for black silk and lace."

"Certainly not," she snapped.

His low chuckle drifted through the empty

streets. "Why, darling, I begin to wonder if you are truly as anxious as you pretend to be my bride."

"Not anxious enough to attire myself as a tart."

"Oh, we shall see."

With athletic ease, Hart vaulted from the carriage and before she could even guess his intent he had spanned her tiny waist with his hands to lift her onto the padded seat he had so recently vacated. It seemed like a good, solid plan until an unmistakable jolt of awareness shot through his body at the lavender heat that briefly surrounded him. Dear God, he thought in dazed amazement, how could he possibly desire this woman with such intensity? Not just lust but a raw, primitive wish to claim her as his own.

The force of his need was nearly enough to bring him to his knees and for a crazed moment his hands lingered as he battled the urge to pull her close and glory in her sweetness. It was Molly who hastily pulled away and scooted along the bench to put a much-needed distance between them. Muttering a low curse, Hart returned to his place and grimly gathered the reins to set the horses in motion.

Gads, someone should take a shovel and hit him over the head. It seemed the only certain means of keeping him from reacting like a lovesick idiot whenever this woman was near.

Allowing the silence to linger until he was certain he was once more in control of himself, Hart at last slowed the team to glance at the woman sitting in stiff annoyance at his side.

His earlier flare of ill humor faded at the delicate profile marred by a decided grimace about the full lips. Molly was not a female to enjoy a gentleman who used such high-handed methods to achieve his goals and he did not doubt she was currently envisioning him stretched upon the rack or roasting over a fire.

"I trust you received the gift that I sent?" he at last murmured.

Rather surprisingly, her icy expression slowly softened and she turned to offer him a rueful smile.

"Yes, indeed and I owe you my thanks. It was very generous of you," she said.

That tightness returned to his chest as he gazed into the melting brown eyes. "It was my foolishness that led to ruining your gloves. The least I could do was replace them," he retorted, unable to keep the faint huskiness from his voice.

"I would say you did more than simply replace them. I have never possessed such beautiful gloves. It was very thoughtful of you."

Hart choked back the urge to reveal just how long and painstaking the process of picking out the numerous gloves had been. That was something he would share with no one beyond his valet who had been prepared to choke him before the matter was all settled.

"I intend to be a very thoughtful husband. As well as generous," he retorted. "As you will soon discover." Pulling the carriage to a halt, Hart gave a nod of his head toward the discreet dress shop just down the street. "Madame Juliet."

Half expecting a squeal of delight at the notion of being adorned by the most famous modiste in London, one who moreover was as rigidly snobbish as her clientele, Hart blinked in surprise when Molly rounded on him with a decided scowl.

"This is not my dressmaker."

He hastily suppressed the urge to smile at the ridiculous comment. He would have to be daft to suppose Juliet was responsible for the sturdy, frustratingly modest gowns that Molly possessed.

"She should be. She is considered the finest seamstress in all of London."

"No doubt she is very talented, but I prefer my own modiste."

Hart's brief flare of amusement faded as he regarded her stubborn expression. What the devil was the matter with her?

"Why?"

There was a moment of silence before Molly grudgingly squared her shoulders. "If you must know, I cannot afford Madame Juliet."

"Afford?" Hart gave a startled frown. "I never presumed that you could. Naturally I will pay for your trousseau."

"No."

"I beg your pardon?"

"I cannot allow you to pay for my clothing."

Hart blinked. And then blinked again. It was a . . . a charade. It had to be. No chit would willingly turn away an entire wardrobe made by the most famous dressmaker in the country. Especially not one who possessed a heart blackened with greed.

"Why ever not? Soon enough I shall be in charge of all your bills."

"Not my trousseau," she insisted.

He gave an impatient click of his tongue. "You are being absurd, Molly."

"Because I know my duty?"

"Because I wish to offer you this as a gift."

Her chin managed to jut out even farther. "It is very generous of you, Hart, but no."

He clenched his hands, quite certain that this woman was simply placed upon this earth to plague him to death.

Dammit, why was she not giddy with joy? Why was she not tumbling out of the carriage in an effort to reach the dress shop? Why was she not doing all the things that would reassure him precisely why he was behaving as a suspicious cad?

"Surely I deserve an explanation?" he demanded tightly.

She folded her hands in her lap as she turned to gaze down the narrow street rather than meet his smoldering eyes.

"Just because I am a heartless fortune hunter does not mean that I cannot possess my share of pride, my lord."

Was that what this was? Simple pride?

"I do not mean to offer you insult, Molly," he said carefully. "I merely desire to please you with pretty gowns and baubles. Most women would be delighted."

"I believe we have already established that I am not at all like most women," she retorted dryly. "Can we please continue down the street? My modiste possesses a small shop upon the corner."

His jaws snapped together. Very well. She was determined to play the role of the innocent. He would simply have to sweeten the bait.

"Perhaps it would be best to order your wardrobe after we are wed, my dear," he announced with a wry smile. "That way there can be no arguments as to who will pay the bills."

Something that might have been relief rippled over her pale features. "If you wish."

"Good." He forced a smile to his lips. "Then we shall continue onward."

"Onward to where?"

"Naturally we must choose a ring for our engagement. My thought was a diamond, but perhaps you prefer rubies?" He reached out to lightly touch her cheek. "And of course a matching necklace and bracelet as a wedding present. I desire you to shimmer with gems as only proper for the Viscountess Woodhart."

He dangled temptation like the forbidden fruit in the Garden of Eden, then waited for her to place the noose about her neck.

And waited. And waited.

At long last, she licked her lips and glanced uneasily over her shoulder. "Actually I think it best that I return to Lady Falker's."

"Return? Why?"

"I . . . I just recalled that I promised to accompany her to visit Mrs. Summerfield."

With a motion that was perilously close to petulant, Hart tossed himself back into the pads of the carriage and glared at his beautiful companion. Well, that was that. He had played his trump card and still the minx refused to reveal her true self.

Either she was the most proficient actress in the world. Or . . . or what? She wasn't a fortune hunter out to steal his inheritance? Despite all evidence to the contrary?

"Bloody hell," he muttered as his head began to ache.

She regarded him in surprise at his less than gentlemanly language. "I beg your pardon?"

"You truly are the most maddening of females."

"Well." Her lips thinned in annoyance. "Is that not rather like the pot calling the kettle black? I will have you know that you are quite maddening yourself."

His gaze skimmed her pale, angelic features, lingering a long moment upon the satin temptation of her mouth. "I will know you, Molly," he swore in low tones. "Before all this is said and done, I will know the very depths of your heart."

There was no mistaking the guarded expression that abruptly shuttered her countenance. "I . . . think we should be on our way."

She was hiding something. There could be no doubt about that.

The question was, what.

Chapter Nine

At precisely midnight, Georgie slipped from the house and made her way through the garden. More than once she paused to hide in the shadows and ensure that there were no servants lurking about to notice her peculiar behavior. She even scrambled behind a bush when she heard the distant call of the Watch.

It was only when she was certain her passage had gone unnoted that she at last let herself through the mews and entered the shadowed stables.

She was being ridiculous, of course. There was no need to act as if she were a thief slipping about her own property. After all, if she decided to visit her stables in the midst of the night it was certainly her right. And to creep about in such a covert manner was bound to create far more suspicion than simply marching through the mews with her head held high.

Unfortunately, she possessed a stunning history of acting the fool. At least when it came to Andrew Conwell, Lord Canfield.

Grimly hiding herself beside the door, Georgie peered into the dark alley.

She had not desired to send her servant to that horrid hovel that Andrew secretly called home. And she certainly had not desired to request that he meet with her in private. Not when they could barely be in each other's presence without that prickling urge to come to blows.

Or kisses . . .

A shiver raced over her skin as she wrapped her arms about her waist. No. She would not allow such dangerous thoughts to even enter her mind.

She had requested Andrew to meet with her for precisely one purpose.

Molly.

There was simply no one else she could depend upon. Despite her best efforts, she had been unable to convince her naive and reckless young friend of her folly. No one dared to cross Lord Woodhart. No one with any sense at least. And now with the added concern that Molly was becoming increasingly fascinated with the wicked gentleman she knew she had to take more drastic measures.

Surely Molly would listen to reason from the older brother that she adored?

"Ah, Georgie. As beautiful as ever." A soft, honey voice whispered from behind.

Already on edge, Georgie nearly leapt from her skin as she whirled about to confront the gentleman leaning negligently against a nearby stall.

In the gloom of the stables it was nearly impossible to make out more than a hard, lean form that was decidedly male. Georgie, however, had no trouble placing her guest. It was in the manner her skin abruptly tingled with goose bumps and in the erratic beat of her heart.

Who needed light to know that the gentleman's hair was the shade of morning sunlight? Or that his features were gratingly perfect from the noble brow and slender nose to the blue eyes that shimmered with mischievous humor. Such things were engraved into her mind and haunted her dreams.

"Andrew." Georgie determinedly gathered her tattered composure. This encounter would be difficult enough without her nerves leaping and jumping like a drunken ballerina. "You startled me."

Shoving himself upright, Andrew slowly strolled to stand directly before her. A shaft of moonlight tumbled over his face to reveal his beautiful male features taut with inner emotions.

"You did send your servant to request that I meet you here this evening, did you not?" he demanded.

"Of course." She smoothed her shaky hands over her skirts. "I simply expected you to appear through the alley."

"Over the past few years I have discovered it far safer to choose the less expected path."

Unwittingly, Georgie's expression thinned with disapproval. "I suppose you have."

Andrew's lips twisted as he folded his arms over his chest. "Ah, there is that rigid condemnation that always warms my heart. You cannot know how I have missed it, darling Georgie."

A pang shot through her heart at the bitter edge to his words. Ridiculous, of course. There was no earthly reason to blame herself for Andrew's downfall. She had been perfectly reasonable two years before to demand that he become the sort of responsible, trustworthy gentleman she desired. What female would wed a rash, impulsive husband that might very well bring them both to ruin?

The fact that he had taken her requests as an insult to his pride and promptly rushed off to London to wallow in his own stupidity had nothing to do with her. Indeed, it only proved she had been right to question his steadfastness.

Unfortunately, it did not keep her from wondering what might have been. What if she had not tossed his proposal back in his face? What if he had stayed in Surrey? What if . . .

She abruptly wrenched herself back to the present. Blast but there was no other man in all of England who could rattle her so.

"I requested that you meet me here to discuss Molly," she reminded him in chilled tones.

He gave a lift of his shoulders. "Well, I did not presume that it was out of any overwhelming desire to resume our torturously ended affair."

She flinched despite her best intentions. "Andrew."

"Forgive me. It is just seeing you . . ." Breaking off his dark words, Andrew shoved his hands through his golden curls and turned to pace across the width of the door before collecting himself enough to face her. "You assured me in your note that Molly was not ill, nor injured. I must presume that she has acquired an unlikely addiction to the gaming tables or she has formed an attachment to some unworthy male."

Forcing herself to concentrate sternly upon her friend and not the tight knots lodged in her stomach, Georgie sucked in a deep breath.

"Perhaps you will not be quite so flippant when you discover she is currently engaged to Lord Woodhart."

There was no mistaking the sharp disbelief that hardened his features. "What?"

"She is determined to get her hands upon Lady Woodhart's inheritance."

"Bloody hell. I warned her. I told her not to even consider playing such a dangerous game."

"She is attempting to help you," Georgie could not resist pointing out.

He gave a low growl at the unnecessary reminder. "Would you like to thrust the dagger a bit deeper, Georgie? I know precisely why my sister is risking her foolish, stubborn neck. It is to save my worthless hide from the consequences of my own stupidity."

Georgie possessed the grace to blush. She was not by nature a spiteful person. Not even toward those who had managed to break her heart.

"I am sorry," she muttered in low tones. "It is only that I am concerned for Molly."

"As am I." An air of purpose settled about him. "Is Lord Woodhart treating her ill? Has he threatened her?"

"Oh, he made a few attempts to bully and frighten her, but Molly refused to be intimidated."

Andrew gave a short, humorless laugh. "That sounds like my Molly."

Georgie gave an unconscious shake of her head. "But now . . ."

"What is it?"

"He claims that he is perfectly prepared to have Molly as his bride."

A thick, disbelieving silence filled the stables before Andrew took a stiff step forward.

"Hart desires Molly as his wife?" he rasped.

"So he says, although Molly is certain that it is nothing but a ploy to ensure she balks. She is quite convinced he will never arrive at the chapel for the ceremony."

"And what do you believe?"

Georgie was caught off guard by his abrupt demand for her opinion. Although she had been in charge of her own household and maintained a rare independence, it had been some time since a gentleman had desired to actually listen to what she had to say. Certainly Lord Falker had never cared what was upon her mind.

Indeed, if she were perfectly honest with herself, she would acknowledge that Andrew was the only man ever to make her feel as if what she had to say mattered.

Forced to clear the lump forming in her throat, Georgie met his concerned gaze.

"I believe that Molly is extraordinarily naive when it comes to gentlemen such as Lord Woodhart. And even more naive when it comes to her own heart," she confessed.

"What do you imply?"

"Whatever his sins Lord Woodhart is a very handsome and charming gentleman. Moreover he knows precisely the means of stirring a young lady's emotions."

His brows snapped together. "You believe she is falling in love with the scoundrel?"

Georgie recalled her friend's blushes and fluttering confusion whenever the name of Lord Woodhart was broached. Such reactions were not those of a maiden who detested or even feared a gentleman.

"I think it is a distinct danger."

Andrew gave a slow shake of his head. "No, surely not. She is too intelligent to be swayed by a handsome countenance and charming smile."

"Intelligence rarely has anything to do with love."

Andrew seemed to still in the shadows, his expression unreadable as he allowed his gaze to sweep over her stiff form.

"I suppose that is true enough, as we know to our sorrow."

A hallow pang of loss wrenched at her heart. "Andrew."

He stepped forward, his fingers reaching out to touch her cheek before she could guess his intentions.

"Do you have any notion of how hard it is to be with you here?" he murmured in husky tones. "To see you and speak with you and yet know you are forever beyond my reach?"

This time her heart did not just wrench, it nearly shattered. Oh Lord, but she would give her soul to turn back the hands of time. To return to the magical days when love had been everything and the future was nothing but a rosy dream.

An impossible, futile dream.

"Please . . . do not," she whispered, unable to force herself to move from his touch.

"I almost did not come. I knew how much it would hurt to be alone with you." His eyes darkened. "Or at least I thought I knew. Nothing could have truly prepared me."

Georgie's lashes fluttered downward as she breathed deeply of his warm, male skin. "Andrew, we are here for Molly."

Just for a moment she half feared, half hoped that he would ignore her soft plea for sanity. Then, with a rasping sigh, his fingers were slipping from her face and he was taking a firm step backward.

"You are right." Scrubbing his hands over his face in a weary motion, Andrew at last lifted his head to regard her with a grimly determined expression. "Do not fear. I will ensure that Molly is not harmed."

Georgie resisted the urge to reach out and trace the lines of worry that marred his features.

"Will you speak with her?"

His lips hardened to a thin line. "I have spoken with her. And warned her. And even threatened her. I shall have to take more drastic measures."

She blinked in surprise at the sudden glimpse of ruthless resolve behind the boyish charm. It reminded her that this was no longer the lighthearted companion of her childhood, but a dangerous stranger who risked his life every evening.

"What will you do?"

"I do not yet know."

Against her will a surge of concern raced through Georgie. Whatever their painful history, she could not forget what they had once meant to one another.

"You must be careful," she warned, reaching out to lightly touch his arm.

Golden brows lifted in obvious surprise. "I am not so far sunk that I would harm my own sister."

She gave an impatient click of her tongue. "I did not believe you would. I merely meant that Lord Woodhart is quite clever. If he should discover your disguise, he might very well ruin you."

In the dim shadows, his features slowly softened and a warm hand shifted to cover her own.

"I will take care," he promised softly.

Sweet, nearly forgotten awareness raced through Georgie's blood. A dangerous awareness she had not felt in a very long time.

Swallowing heavily, she took an abrupt step back. "I must go."

"Georgie." His hand reached out as if he would attempt to halt her, but as he encountered her wary gaze he slowly allowed his arm to drop. "Of course. Good night and good-bye, my dear."

With the elegance that was so much a part of him, Andrew swept her a deep bow before turning on his heel and disappearing in the darkness between the stalls.

For long moments, Georgie stood by the door in troubled silence. She had known this meeting would be difficult. Even painful.

What she had not expected was the bittersweet

pleasure of simply being near the gentleman she still loved.

The modest gathering at Lady Sinclair's should have proven to be a welcome distraction. It did, after all, have the good fortune to attract several of the more brilliant political figures and war heroes. There were even a spattering of poets and explorers among the glittering throng.

Oddly, however, despite the intellectual conversations and charming flirtations, Molly discovered herself restless and even a tad bored.

It had nothing to do with the fact that Lord Woodhart was not in attendance, she was swift to reassure herself. Of course it wasn't. The man was a plague and a pest.

It was only that her nerves were ravaged by her dangerous game. And of course, the fact that Hart was clearly attempting to drive her batty.

Why else would he behave as a bully one day, a seductive charmer the next and then without warning a vulnerable suitor who desired nothing more than to please her?

Worse of all he had once again disappeared, leaving her in constant dread of when he might suddenly slip up behind her and toss her world into chaos.

Who could blame her for skulking in the shadows and counting the moments until she could politely take her leave?

At last disgusted with herself, Molly covertly edged her way past the mingling crowd and slipped through the door to the wide terrace.

Perhaps a few moments alone would allow her to thrust aside the unwelcome thoughts of her fiancé and allow her to endure the remainder of the evening with a measure of peace. If nothing else, she would be away from the chatter that was beginning to make her head ache.

Avoiding the handful of couples bracing the winter breeze to enjoy a few moments alone, Molly paused beside a flickering torch. It was a reasonably isolated spot to gather her thoughts.

Or at least it seemed reasonably isolated.

She had barely managed to draw in a deep breath when there was the sound of approaching footsteps and a very large, very male form was hovering beside her.

"Hair of spun gold, eyes of a Mediterranean night and the features of an angel," a dark voice whispered near her ear. "You must be Miss Conwell."

With a startled jerk, Molly was spinning about to glare at the gentleman who was standing far too close for propriety. Just for the briefest of moments, she thought it was Hart and her breath caught in her throat. Then, the torch flickered and she realized that while the hard, beautiful features were very much like Hart's there were enough subtle differences to prove that this was indeed a stranger.

"Sir." Conjuring her most disapproving expression, Molly took a deliberate step backward. "I do not believe we have been introduced."

"Ah, a tragedy that must be corrected at once," the man drawled, offering a half bow. "I am Thorpe."

Her brows drew together. "Thorpe?"

He waved an indolent hand. "Oh, I do possess

a ponderous list of titles and names that are far too tedious to rattle off. Thorpe is far more . . . intimate."

Sensing a danger prickling in the air that she did not understand, Molly clutched her fan in a tight grip. It wasn't much of a weapon, but it was the only one she possessed. And she wasn't afraid to use it.

"Too intimate for mere strangers, sir."

A hard, rather unpleasant glitter entered his midnight eyes. "But we are not strangers, my dear. At least we very soon will not be. After Christmas we will be family. Does that not just send a shiver of delight through your heart?"

It sent a shiver of something through her heart, but she was fairly certain it was not delight.

Swallowing heavily, she attempted to disguise her racing heart. "You are related to Lord Woodhart?"

"Devoted, if sometimes rather testy and blood-thirsty, cousins."

Well, that certainly explained the fact they could pass as twins. Unfortunately, it did not explain why he would seek her out.

"I see. Is there something you desire?"

His slow smile was far more threatening than any frown could ever be. "You."

Her? A tingle inched down her spine. She was fairly certain he did not mean that as a compliment.

Not when he was regarding her as if she were some loathsome insect that he longed to squash.

"I must return to Lady Falker," she muttered.

Without warning, his hand shot out to grasp her upper arm. "Surely there is no hurry?"

Molly wetted her suddenly dry lips. His grip was not painful, but it was firm enough to warn her that he had no intention of letting her slip away.

"She will be concerned if she notes that I am not in the ballroom," she warned in stiff tones. "I would not wish her to create a scene in searching for me."

"No, we most certainly do not desire an ugly scene," he drawled in return.

"Then please release me."

His grip merely tightened. "Actually Lady Falker will not be at all concerned with your absence."

"I beg your pardon?"

"I possessed the foresight to ensure that she is properly distracted by Mrs. Milton," he revealed. "The woman is as tenacious as a leech and just as difficult to dislodge. It should be some time before Lady Falker even notices you are absent."

Her spine stiffened at his audacity. "I . . . how dare you?"

"Quite easily." With a firm tug, Thorpe had her stumbling toward the nearby steps leading to the gardens. "Shall we take a stroll?"

Managing to regain her balance as she was ruthlessly steered forward, Molly flashed her captor a jaundiced glare.

"Do I have a choice?"

"None whatsoever."

Her teeth clenched in annoyance. "I see that beastly manners and utter arrogance is a family trait."

Surprisingly, her words elicited nothing more than a low chuckle from her companion.

"Delightful, is it not?"

"Delightful was not quite the word I would use."

"I am sure it is not."

Realizing that the annoying man was quite as impervious to insult as his cousin, Molly set her chin to a stubborn angle.

"Why are you doing this?" she demanded.

"It is nothing overly nefarious," he drawled. "I merely wish to have a word in private with you."

Her gaze narrowed. "Did Hart send you?"

He appeared genuinely startled by her question. "Gads, no. I do not doubt he will have my head upon a platter when he discovers I have even approached you. Here we are." At last reaching the sunken rose garden complete with a Italian marble fountain, Thorpe came to a halt and glanced about his surroundings. "Lovely. I will give Lady Sinclair credit. For all her lack of blue blood she does possess an exquisite taste in gardens."

Confused, and not at all in the humor to mind her manners, Molly jerked her arm free of his lingering grasp.

"Since as a rule it is those without proper blue blood who actually put their hands in the dirt to create such a garden, I would think her lack of aristocracy was quite an asset."

The raven brows rose in a manner disturbingly familiar. "Good heavens, Miss Conwell, do not tell me that the daughter of a Baron, one who moreover is about to wed a very large fortune, actually believes in the nonsense of all being created as equal?"

It was precisely what she believed, but knowing

that she was merely being goaded, Molly turned to the gentleman squarely.

"Are you truly curious of my political beliefs?"

"Perhaps under different circumstances. Now, however, my only interest is in Hart."

"I do not know where he is, if that is what you desire. Indeed I have not seen him for the past week."

Thorpe folded his arms over his chest, peering down the long length of his nose. "I am not concerned with his whereabouts. I am concerned with his future."

Ah. So now they were to come to the crux of the matter. Molly silently girded herself for the undoubted battle.

"You believe that Lord Woodhart is incapable of seeing to his own future?"

"Not when he is allowing himself to be befuddled by a beautiful woman."

Beautiful woman? Molly blinked in shock. Was the man daft or simply blind?

"I assure you, I most certainly have not befuddled your cousin, sir," she retorted in wary tones. "I could not even if I desired too."

"Do not be so modest, my dear. Not only do you possess an undoubted allure, but there is an innocence about you that is bound to tug the heart of a susceptible gentleman."

"Susceptible gentleman?" A short laugh was wrenched from her throat. "Surely you do not refer to the Heartless Viscount?"

A hard, humorless smile curled his lips. "He is not nearly so heartless as he would have others believe. Victoria's treachery merely made him create the illusion he could no longer be hurt by others."

The righteous anger and dislike for being threatened by a complete stranger abruptly faltered as she regarded Thorpe with a gathering frown.

"Do you speak of the maiden he left standing at the altar?"

There was a moment's pause as Thorpe regarded her pale features with a searching intensity.

"That is the story put out by Victoria and her family. One that Hart never bothered to correct." The lean features hardened with a chilled anger. "The truth of the matter is that Hart caught his beloved fiancée in a disgustingly compromising position mere hours before the wedding. After assuring Victoria he would have himself hanged before going through the marriage, he disappeared from London for weeks to battle his disillusionment."

Molly bit her bottom lip until she drew blood. Damn and blast this man. From the beginning, she had sought to convince herself that Hart was no more than a ruthless libertine who was without conscience or morals. Even when she had witnessed glimmers of his tender charm and staunchly guarded vulnerability she had battled to remain blind.

How else was she to treat him as the enemy? How else could she ease her own conscience at taking money that truly did not belong to her?

Now Thorpe was forcing her to consider her fiancé as a man wounded by his past and wary of being hurt once again. A man, moreover, undeserving of paying for the sins of Andrew.

Abruptly spinning away from the probing gaze that silently watched the emotions flicker over her countenance, Molly pressed her hands to her heaving stomach.

"I . . . did not know," she muttered.

"He was frankly devastated by the realization his trust had been so ruthlessly violated." Thorpe pressed his dagger deeper. "It took him months to recover from the blow and even now he keeps himself isolated in a manner I find worrisome."

"Why are you telling me this?"

"Oh, it is not to gain your sympathy, if that is what you fear," he mocked. "Hart assures me that you have none. I only wish to reveal my deep concern for my cousin. I refuse to stand aside and allow him to be hurt and disappointed once again."

Molly squeezed shut her eyes at his condemning tone. Why shouldn't he be condemning, she chastised herself? To his mind she was no better than a common thief.

And at this moment, she wasn't certain he was not right.

"I suppose you intend to threaten me now?" she challenged in husky tones.

"On the contrary, Miss Conwell," he retorted. "I intend to make you a very happy woman."

Decidedly alarmed by the unexpected words, Molly turned to eye the towering gentleman with a suspicious gaze.

"What do you mean?"

His eyes glittered as cold as a winter night. "I

am willing to offer you a bank draft for thirty thousand pounds if you will swear to leave London and never trouble Hart again."

Her mouth went dry as she took an instinctive step backward. "Why? Why would you do such a thing?"

"I assure you that it is a small price to pay to ensure that Hart is not once again butchered by a ruthless jade."

Molly flinched as if she had been physically struck. In truth, she would have preferred a solid slap. It would not have been nearly so painful as the vicious words that cut deep into her heart.

A ruthless jade.

Was that what she had become?

In her madness to save her brother had she become what she most detested?

Muffling a low groan, Molly abruptly hiked up her skirts and fled from the taunting gentleman. She could not think clearly. Not with him glaring at her as if she were some appalling rodent.

She needed time alone to gather her rattled senses. Perhaps then she wouldn't be wishing she could leap off the nearest cliff.

Chapter Ten

Hart had not intended to attend the elegant ball. What was the purpose? All his devious plots and schemes had come to naught. Unless, of course, he counted their stunning achievement in making him more confused and uncertain than ever.

It did not seem to matter how hard he tried he could not force Molly into the mold of a heartless vixen.

Oh, there was no doubt she was determined to get her hands upon his grandmother's inheritance. She was as tenacious as a leech when it came to bleeding him of his fortune.

But even while his common sense demanded that he accept she was without conscience or morals, his heart refused to accept the obvious.

There were simply too many contradictions. Her unwitting displays of kindness, her utter innocence, her refusal to accept lavish gifts. They all revealed a maiden who was incapable of deliberately deceiving another.

Or the fact that he was flirting with madness once again.

Besieged with a restless need to be near Molly

regardless of her unsettlingly influence upon his emotions, Hart had at last given into the inevitable. Attiring himself in a pristine black coat and white pantaloons, he had directed his driver to the Mayfair townhouse.

Once he arrived, however, he was disgruntled to discover that Molly was not among the chattering crowd. Odd considering that Lady Falker's maid had assured Carter just that morning that the ladies would be attending.

With a growing unease, he searched through the various rooms and at last weaved his way to the French doors and onto the terrace. He entered the gardens just in time to witness Molly's flurry of silken flight.

Caught off guard, he could only watch as she disappeared into the shadows at the back of the townhouse. Then slowly, his gaze narrowed as he turned his attention to the tall, elegantly familiar form of Lord Thorpe.

Obviously, Molly was upset. And he could easily guess the cause of her hasty flight.

With long strides, he made his way down the stairs and moved to stand directly behind his cousin.

"What the devil were you doing with Molly?" he growled, unaware that he was revealing far too much concern for a woman he had branded a fortune hunter.

Stiffening at the abrupt intrusion, Thorpe took a moment before he turned to confront his bristling relative.

"Good Lord, Hart," he drawled with his usual nonchalance. "Has no one taught you that it is extremely rude to lurk about and startle a gentleman out of his wits?"

"You did not answer my question." Hart took a smooth step closer. "Why were you out here with Molly?"

Thorpe shrugged. "I merely wished to have a word in private with her."

"Why?"

"Curiosity, I suppose." Thorpe folded his arms across his chest, his lips twisting into a humorless smile. "She has managed to lead you about like a trained monkey. I desired to discover the source of her bewitchment."

Having known Thorpe a lifetime, Hart easily recognized the ploy. His cousin was attempting to distract him.

"And all you did was speak with her?" he pressed grimly.

A raven brow arched. "Did you think I lured her out here for a spot of seduction?"

Thankfully such a thought had never occurred to him. A fortunate thing for his bothersome relative. It might very well have earned a sharp poke to the nose.

"I think that she fled from you as if she were terrified," he accused. "I cannot help but wonder why."

A guarded expression descended upon the handsome male features. "Who can say? Females as a point of honor are odd, unpredictable creatures."

True enough, but Hart was quite certain that Molly's distress was more than simple female fickleness.

"Did you threaten her?" he demanded.

Thorpe regarded him steadily. "Would it trouble you if I did?"

"I do not want you involved."

"And that is all that bothers you?"

"Of course."

"It could not be that you are concerned that I might have upset Miss Conwell?" his cousin charged.

Well certainly he was damned well concerned, Hart grumpily acknowledged. To think of Molly being hurt or frightened was enough to make his blood run hot. Still, it did not seem entirely wise to confess such a dangerous reaction. Not when poor Thorpe was already consumed with worry for his sanity.

"This is between Molly and myself," he instead insisted, his tone revealing his refusal to argue the point. "I do not want you interfering."

Thorpe gave a slow shake of his head. "Hart, you are playing a dangerous game."

Hart clenched his hands at his side. No one knew better than him the dangers of this particular game. Or the consequences of losing it.

"It is my game to play," he retorted. "And without the assistance of a busybody relative."

Confident he had made his point, Hart turned on his heel and set a path to follow Molly. He was quite certain he was the last person she desired to see at the moment, but he could not allow her to believe that he had requested Thorpe bully and intimidate her.

Why that bothered him so deeply was a question he did not wish to ponder at the moment.

Moving through the shadows, he traced his way along the back of the house, pausing at the various doors until he at last discovered one that led to a secluded library. Peering within he could just make out the slender form of Molly leaning against a bookcase with her back to him. In the heavy silence, he could hear the muffled sound of sobbing.

A sharp, unfamiliar pain ripped through his heart as he hesitantly entered the room.

"Molly?"

In the dusky shadows, he could sense her freeze in shock at his unexpected appearance. He was also conscious of her furtive effort to wipe away the evidence of her distress.

So, she was a maiden who did not use tears as a weapon. Yet another revelation.

"Please . . . go away," she muttered in husky tones.

"I cannot do that." Closing the door behind him, Hart slid the lock into place before moving forward. "You are upset."

"Do not be absurd." She squared her shoulders although she was careful not to turn about. "I merely desired a few moments alone."

"Molly, I know you were in the gardens with Thorpe. What did he say to you?"

"Does it matter?"

It should not. He had struggled for weeks to find her weaknesses and to use them to his advantage. Now she seemed to be utterly vulnerable and all he could think about was finding some means to ease her pain.

"You are my fiancée," he lamely uttered.

"Fah." Reluctantly she turned to face him, her countenance still damp from tears. "We both know that you consider our engagement no more than a charade."

Did he? He was not nearly so certain as he should be.

"And we both know that a heartless fortune hunter would not be reduced to tears by a few unkind words," he retorted gently. "I begin to wonder if we are both frauds, my sweet."

Surprisingly, his words produced a deep scowl as she folded her arms about her waist. "Blast you, do not do that."

Hart lifted his brows in puzzlement. "Do what?"

"Be kind to me."

Thorpe was right, he silently conceded. Females were odd, unpredictable creatures. With a healthy dose of contrariness thrown in for the bargain.

"You would rather I be unkind?" he demanded.

"Yes." She gave a restless shrug. "You are supposed to be the enemy."

Hart stilled at the peculiar words. "Why am I the enemy, Molly?"

She bit her lip, almost as if she had given away more than she intended. "You have treated me abominably."

Well, he could hardly deny her accusation. He had treated her abominably. Perhaps more abominably than she truly deserved.

He shoved impatient fingers through his hair, not at all comfortable revealing his most private feelings.

"I will admit that I have never trusted you or

your motives in befriending my grandmother. I did not want her hurt." He paused before giving a grim laugh. "Or perhaps it was myself that I feared might be hurt."

Her wary expression softened at his grudging confession. "You believe all women are untrustworthy because Miss Darlington betrayed you?"

Hart jerked in surprise at her soft question. Good God, how the devil had she learned that he was betrayed? No one knew the truth of Victoria. Well, no one but his interfering, aggravating cousin.

His features thinned with annoyance as he folded his arms over his chest.

"Ah, I suppose I must thank Thorpe for revealing my sordid past. I will make sure to share my appreciation when next we meet."

Her hand impulsively reached out as if to touch him before being drawn sharply back. "Do not be angry with him. He is merely concerned for you. Families are meant to care for one another."

"Caring for and interfering are two different matters. What did he tell you?"

"Only that you were betrayed and that you have not yet fully recovered."

Hart shuddered in horror. How could his cousin reveal his secrets? Especially to Molly. He knew just how embarrassing Hart found Victoria's defection.

"So, I am not only a cuckolded fool, but doddy in the bargain. Lovely," he muttered in harsh tones.

Astonishingly, her brows snapped together as if she were angered by his response. "That is absurd."

"What?"

"Miss Darlington is the fool, not you," she informed him sternly. "You offered her an honorable position as your wife and she chose to behave in a manner befitting a tart."

It was the same words he had heard from Thorpe over and over. Still, he had certainly never expected to hear them from a woman who was supposed to be without a heart or conscience. One who moreover confessed from her own sweet lips that she considered him the enemy.

"I was the blind idiot who refused to realize that her affections were not sincere."

"You cannot blame yourself."

"Actually, I can. Quite easily."

Her frown eased slightly as she tilted her head to one side. "Is that the reason you allowed others to believe you jilted her rather than explaining the truth?"

Hart shifted uneasily, not certain why he was even discussing his past with this maiden. Certainly, he had never shared his thoughts or emotions of that horrid time before. But for once it seemed important to make someone understand.

No, he wryly conceded. Not someone. Molly. Just Molly.

He sighed as his hand shifted to rub the back of his neck. "It was preferable to having the entire *ton* chuckling over the fact I was a gullible romantic."

There was a brief silence before Molly stepped forward, her gaze sweeping his tense countenance.

"She harmed you a great deal," she said softly.

His heart gave an odd leap. "It is all in the past."

"No." She shook her head. "It still haunts you. Otherwise you would not be so wary of others."

Slowly, so as not to alarm her, Hart reached out to lightly brush a golden curl that lay against her temple.

"Do you refer to yourself?" he demanded. "Do you seek my trust?"

She appeared caught off guard by his question as she abruptly pulled from his touch and turned her back upon him.

"I . . . no. I do not ask for your trust," she muttered.

Hart frowned, feeling as if he were standing upon a quagmire. With every step he took closer to this female he discovered himself being pulled further away.

"Molly?"

She pressed her hands to her face. "This is wrong."

"What is wrong?" Moving forward, he firmly turned her about and pulled her into his arms. There was something deeply troubling her. Something that was making her behave in a manner that was contrary to her true self. He was now certain of it. And he had to discover what it was. If only for his own sanity. "Tell me."

"I cannot." She placed her hands upon his chest but did not attempt to break his hold. "Please, I must go."

His eyes briefly closed at the sweetness that raced through him at having her so near. To even think that he might soon never know such pleasure again was nearly unbearable.

"No. Tell me what it is you are hiding."

"Hart," she whispered in broken tones.

He summoned a faint smile as he studied her pale countenance. "I bared my sordid secrets. And in truth it was surprisingly painless."

She licked her lips as a tremor swept through her slender form. "My secrets . . . they . . ."

"What?"

"They are not mine to share."

Hart stilled. Who was she protecting? Her parents were dead and her brother playing the libertine in Europe. A friend? Or . . . could it be a lover?

No. She was too innocent to have given her heart or her body to another, his heart fiercely whispered. Far more innocent than Victoria could ever have hoped to be.

"But these secrets do include the reason you are determined to hold onto my grandmother's fortune?"

Something that might have been pain darkened her eyes as her hands unwittingly clutched at the lapels of his coat.

"No more," she pleaded. "We must leave before we are discovered."

Her words should have sent a jolt of panic through him. Engaged or not the tattlers would delight in spreading tales of them locked alone together in a darkened room. Tales that would demand a swift marriage.

What he felt, however, was only a deepening need to keep her close to him.

"If we are discovered, then it will only ensure

that our marriage will take place," he pointed out. "That is what you desire, is it not?"

Her agitation was nearly palpable as she turned her head to gaze into the shadows. "I no longer know what I desire. It was so clear in the beginning, and now you have managed to confuse and befuddle me until I cannot gather my wits."

"Good," he said with undeniable relish.

Her gaze sharply returned to study his pleased expression. "Good?"

"I should not wish to be alone in my befuddlement."

"You befuddled?" She offered a disgruntled tsk. "Fah. You are always in utter command."

He reached out to take her hand and placed it against his racing heart. It was one truth she could not deny.

"If I were in utter command, then why would Thorpe risk my wrath to corner you in the garden?"

A sad expression flitted over her expressive features. "People do odd, sometimes insane things when they feel someone they love is being threatened."

Being threatened? Was someone she loved in danger? That would certainly explain a great deal.

"People such as you?"

If he hoped to catch her off guard, he was in for a disappointment as the wariness he detested returned.

"Has anyone told you that you can be annoyingly insistent?" she charged.

"I want to understand."

"Hart, it is impossible."

"Only if you make it so."

"No."

With unexpected strength, she was pulling from his grasp and fleeing for the door. Hart stumbled and before he could recover, she was already out of the room and heading for the ballroom.

Cursing himself for allowing a chit that he could hold in one hand to escape, Hart shoved his fingers through his hair. He was still no closer to discovering what had led Molly to her dangerous charade. Or if he could devise some means to help her.

All he had truly learned was that he could no more allow Miss Molly Conwell to disappear from his life than he could force his heart to stop beating.

It was not until Molly was mere steps from the ballroom that she came to a halt and made a futile effort to smooth her decidedly mussed appearance.

With shaky hands, she wiped the last traces of tears from her cheeks and smoothed the curls that had strayed from the tidy knot atop her head. She did not doubt that she looked as if she had been cavorting in the gardens, or even scooping out the stables, but at the moment she was far more concerned with discovering Georgie and convincing her to return home than what the scandalmongers might think.

She felt sick. Sick to her stomach. Sick in her soul. And sick at heart.

Hart was supposed to be a monster. Someone she could trick and deceive without guilt.

But instead he was simply a man who had been deeply wounded once before and now sought to protect himself from those who would once again offer him pain.

Someone like herself.

A wave of nausea swirled through her stomach and giving up the impossible task of hiding her distress, Molly stepped among the crowd and battled her way toward the distant refreshment table. Halfway there she spotted Georgie standing by herself near a fluted column.

Barely keeping herself from rushing toward her friend like a hoyden, Molly managed to keep her steps steady until she at last reached Georgie's side.

Turning, Lady Falker offered a relieved smile at her appearance. "There you are. I have been . . ." Abruptly noticing Molly's reddened nose and still wet lashes, she grasped her arm and pulled her into a shallow alcove. "What has occurred?"

Still shaky and a breath away from sobbing like a baby, Molly knew she could not possibly explain the disturbing confrontations at this moment. It would take several hours to calm down enough to sort through her confusion of emotions.

"It is nothing."

Georgie frowned. "A nothing that has made you cry. I can only presume that Lord Woodhart is involved."

"I do not wish to discuss this now, Georgie. Can we please just go home?"

"Of course." With a brisk efficiency, Georgie was steering her along the edge of the crowd and toward the door. "Damn, I could throttle that horrid man," she muttered beneath her breath.

"Do not blame Lord Woodhart." Molly could not help but defend the gentleman who was lodged far too deeply into her heart. "I am the one who created this mess."

She sensed her friend's sharp glance. "That does not excuse his wretched behavior."

"Actually it excuses a great deal," she said softly.

"Molly?"

"Please, not now."

Although she no doubt longed to press for answers, Georgie was sensitive enough to Molly's fragile state to hold her tongue. Even when they had taken their departure and climbed into the carriage, Georgie was careful to keep her chatter upon inconsequential matters.

Once at home, Molly muttered a hasty good night before heading toward the stairs. Not turning about she missed her friend motioning for a waiting footman and whispering anxiously in his ear.

All she knew was that she had never felt so lost and alone in her life.

Chapter Eleven

Hart forced himself to begin his day like any other despite the fact he had devoted the night to restlessly brooding upon his latest confrontation with Molly.

What the devil was the sense in lying abed like some lovesick goon, he sternly chided himself? Not only would he feel like a damnable fool, but it would accomplish nothing more than worrying his servants and giving the *ton* fodder for gossip.

Besides which he was far too agitated to sedately remain locked in his chambers.

And so with an effort he quietly allowed himself to be bathed and dressed by his valet, even going so far as to indulge in his usual morning wrangling with Carter over his choice in waistcoats.

Once suitably groomed, he made his way to the library where he absently flipped through the morning papers before tossing them aside and making a dismal effort at attending to his vast business concerns. A very dismal effort he discovered as he totaled his ledgers for the sixth time only to arrive at the sixth different sum. Obviously, he was doing no more than making a muck of the accounts and with an impatient click of his tongue he pushed them aside and headed for the breakfast room.

Bloody hell, surely he could manage to eat without utter mishap?

Seating himself at the head of the table, Hart allowed the waiting footman to fill his plate with savory ham and several slices of toast. He was, however, wise enough to avoid the scalding tea that was certain to be disaster on such a morning and instead motioned for the rich burgundy wine that he preferred.

Nearly an hour later, he polished off the last of his ham and sat back with a sigh. He had hoped a full stomach might somehow settle his tangled nerves. Clearly a futile hope, he concluded as his fingers impatiently tapped upon the table and his thoughts continued to return time and time again to the aggravating female who had stormed his defenses and left him reeling with the impact.

It was a decided relief when Carter entered the room and offered a well-needed distraction.

"Pardon me, my lord," the valet murmured with a faint bow.

Forcing himself to raise a lazy brow, Hart tossed aside his linen napkin. "Ah, Carter, I suppose you have come to argue over my choice in waistcoats once again. I tell you I refuse to wear an insipid shade of pink with this delightful coat."

"No, sir. It is a somewhat . . . delicate matter."

It was as much Carter's tone as his words that set Hart on instant alert. Something was wrong. Something that he did not wish to discuss before the other servants.

Careful to keep his casual demeanor, Hart slowly rose to his feet. "More delicate than my waistcoat? Good Lord, you have me aquiver with curiosity." Lifting a slender hand, he motioned toward the silent footman. "That will be all, Smith."

"Yes, my lord." With a bow the servant left the room and closed the door behind his retreating form.

Once alone Hart took several quick steps toward his valet. "What is it, Carter?"

Never easily ruffled, Carter straightened his jacket and cleared his throat before answering.

"As you requested I made my morning call upon Lady Falker's maid."

Hart's heart crashed violently against his chest. "What has occurred? Is Molly hurt?"

"To the best of my knowledge Miss Conwell is in perfect health," Carter was swift to reassure.

Fierce relief shuddered through his body. Anything could be solved so long as Molly was well.

"Then what is it?"

"While I was hiding among the shadows, I noted a carriage near Lady Falker's mews."

Hart blinked, not quite certain what had his servant in a twit. "That is hardly unusual."

"The carriage was unmarked and the windows covered with heavy curtains," Carter clarified. "Also the supposed groom was without livery and looked more a cutthroat than a servant."

Hart frowned. He began to comprehend his valet's suspicions. Despite the fact that several families owned carriages that did not sport a family crest, they did insist upon grooms complete with livery. And of course, what sort of person would hide behind closed curtains in the middle of morning?

"You fear they might be ruffians or thieves?" he demanded, well aware that even the streets of Mayfair were never entirely safe. Not from the desperate.

"It is a definite possibility."

Hart reached out to grasp his valet's shoulder. "Thank you for coming to me."

A faintly concerned expression marred the thin countenance. "My lord, what do you intend to do?"

A grim smile touched Hart's lips. "I am off to remove the rubbish from Lady Falker's mews."

As Hart turned to leave, Carter reached out to touch his sleeve. "My lord."

Turning about, Hart regarded his companion with a lift of his brows. "Yes?"

"Do take care."

He gave a slow nod, knowing just how devoted this man was to him. "I will take the greatest of care," he promised.

Only a handful of blocks away, Molly awoke in little better condition than Hart. Perhaps even worse.

She not only was battling her growing guilt in connection to her treatment of Hart, but she also had to consider what would happen to her brother if she turned from her current path.

Could she live with herself knowing that she had possessed the ability to save him from disaster and had turned her back upon it? What if he were captured as a criminal? Or worse, killed?

Then again, could she accept deceiving and manipulating Hart simply to rescue her brother from his own muddle? It was not after all his fault that Andrew had tossed away his fortune.

Oddly, there had also been hours devoted to mulling over Lady Woodhart and her reasons for making the ridiculous will in the first place.

If she had desired Molly to have a portion of her fortune, why had she not simply left her a straightforward settlement? Why force two people who she knew could barely share a civil word into marriage?

Unless the cunning old woman had realized that beneath all the sparks and bristling that there could be more than mere dislike.

That was a thought she found more than a bit unnerving.

Could she have possibly harbored feelings for Hart from the very beginning? Was that why she had so desperately sought to think of him in the worse possible light?

Ack . . . it was all so jumbled and confusing it was enough to make her poor head throb.

Rising with great reluctance, Molly covertly slipped through the silent townhouse and made her way to the back parlor. She felt in great need for peace and quiet to contemplate what was to be done next.

Or as her old nanny would say, "to stew in her own juices . . ."

Settling in a window seat overlooking the rose garden, Molly wavered from one resolution to

another as she absently shredded her favorite
handkerchief into tatters. She was so lost in
thought that she did not even note the door
being pushed hesitantly open and the pretty
brunette entering the room to regard her with a
guarded expression.

It was not until Georgie at last cleared her
throat that she realized that she was no longer
alone. Turning about she slowly rose to her feet.

"Georgie," she said in surprise.

"Good morning, my dear." Her friend smiled
although it did not seem to reach her eyes. Odd,
that.

"I thought you had already left for your morning calls."

With a fluttery motion, Georgie smoothed her
hands over her lavender skirts. "I fear I am uncon-
scionably late and now I recall that I commanded
the servants to give the attics a thorough cleaning.
It really is most annoying."

Wondering why her friend was behaving in
such a peculiar manner, Molly took a step forward.

"Is there anything I can do to assist?"

"Well, I do hate to ask, but could you possibly
dash out to the stables and tell the groom to
have the carriage brought round in quarter of
an hour?"

Molly blinked. Not so much at the request although that was peculiar enough, but by the
distinct sense that Georgie was hiding something
from her.

Still, what secret could the Lady Falker be attempting to conceal?

She was wealthy, widowed and perfectly free to do as she might choose.

With a metal shrug, she thrust aside the niggling concern. Goodness knew she had enough to trouble her mind without sticking her nose in where it did not belong.

"Of course," she agreed, heading for the door. "You are a dear."

"'Tis no problem."

"Molly."

Halting at the door, Molly turned her head to meet her friend's darkened gaze. "Yes?"

"I . . . nothing. I shall speak with you later."

"Very well."

Leaving the parlor, Molly made her way down the servant's stairs and through the kitchen to the gardens. The sun was shining for the first time in days but without a cape she discovered the wind unpleasantly sharp and wrapping her arms about herself she scampered down the path to the mews. Blast, she should no doubt return to her chambers and fetch a shawl, but now she was on her way she only wanted to be done with her task.

Pressing onward, Molly kept her head lowered as she passed through the gate and toward the stables. She had managed to take half a dozen steps before she heard a rustle behind her and then without warning a pair of ruthless arms wrapped about her.

Her scream ripped through the air until a thick hand clapped over her mouth and muffled her cry for help. At the same moment she was lifted from her feet and smoothly hauled toward the black carriage she had ridiculously failed to notice.

Consumed by a wave of fear and more than a hint of anger, Molly struggled against the firm grip. A futile gesture, of course. Her attacker was not only large, but possessed the sort of bulging muscles that could easily squash her.

Who the devil could be responsible for such an outlandish kidnapping?

She had no money to offer. She was not even wearing jewels that might have tempted a desperate criminal.

Blithely ignoring her desperate kicks and attempts to sink her teeth into the beefy fingers, her captor relentlessly carried her forward, only pausing when he reached the side of the carriage. There was a moment's pause before the door was pushed open from within and she was being bundled into the shadows of the vehicle.

Landing upon the padded bench, Molly shakily brushed back the curls that had tumbled into her eyes and regarded the male form seated across from her. With the windows covered it was difficult to make out more than a vague outline, but even as she shuddered in fear the man leaned forward and her breath caught in disbelieving shock.

"Andrew . . ." She pressed a hand to her racing heart. "Dear God, you nearly scared me out of my wits."

"I am sorry, Molly," her brother retorted although there appeared to be a startling lack of contrition upon his shadowed countenance. "But I preferred to handle the situation without any tedious wrangling."

More than a bit disgruntled by her rough treatment and the fright she had been given, Molly flounced back in her seat. She would have further to say on her brother's wretched behavior, but for now she was more concerned with why he would risk exposure to come and see her.

"What situation? What has occurred?"

His brows drew together as he regarded her with a stern expression. "You know quite well what has occurred. I warned you to have nothing to do with Lord Woodhart, but you chose to flaunt my commands."

Molly gave a small jerk of surprise, certainly not expecting this. "How did you discover . . ."

"Does it matter?" Andrew interrupted.

"As a matter of fact it does." Molly frowned peevishly. For a woman who had been left to fend for herself over the past two years, she was forced to endure a great deal of interference from arrogant gentlemen lately. "I am becoming weary of others somehow knowing my private concerns."

"Perhaps others would stay out of your private concerns if you possessed enough sense to stay out of trouble."

The sheer injustice of the charge made Molly's jaw drop.

"You are hardly in the position to lecture me, Andrew Conwell," she snapped in annoyance.

His expression hardened. "It is precisely because I have made such a muck of my life that I do dare. I will not allow you to sacrifice your future on this dangerous scheme."

"You will not allow?"

The blue gaze swept over her stiff features before his expression softened an he reached out to gently grasp her hand.

"Molly, I do not have much left, but I do have my pride. How do you think it makes me feel to know you are risking everything because of my own stupidity? That because I cannot solve my own problems you are constantly forced to sacrifice yourself?"

Her bristling anger disappeared as swiftly as dew beneath a morning sun. Biting her bottom lip, she battled back the unexpected threat of tears.

Gads, how difficult and confusing this all was.

All she had ever wanted to do was help.

Instead she had only seemed to cause pain and distress for all involved.

"Actually, you need not have risked coming to London, Andrew," she said softly. "I have already begun to have second thoughts."

Expecting him to pleased, or at least relieved, Molly was caught off guard when her brother merely gave a slow shake of his head.

"I wish I could believe you, Molly."

"What?"

He met her gaze steadily. "You have lied to me before concerning Lord Woodhart."

A flare of heat touched her cheeks at the accusation. An accusation that scraped dangerously close to the truth.

"I did not lie," she attempted to hedge. "I . . . simply did not confess my intentions."

Not surprisingly, Andrew appeared spectacularly unimpressed with her logic. A typical male. He could twist the truth any way he desired, but heaven help her if she attempted to skirt it a tad. Well, perhaps she had skirted it more than a tad, she had to concede. Maybe it was more like a wide, gaping berth.

Still, her heart had been in the right place. Hadn't it?

"You know quite well that you led me to believe you would not pursue your reckless plan."

"Perhaps," she grudgingly conceded. "But I assure you that on this occasion that . . ." Molly broke off her words as the carriage suddenly swayed as if it were being pushed from the side, followed by the distinct sound of a scuffle just outside. "What was that?"

Andrew snapped his brows together as he reached for the door. "I haven't the least notion."

His hand had barely reached the handle when the door was thrust open from without and a familiar dark-haired lord was visible in the sudden flood of sunlight.

"Hart?" Molly breathed in disbelief.

Half leaning into the carriage, Hart reached out a hand toward her. "Dear God, Molly, are you harmed?"

"No, of course not. What are you doing here?"

His dark gaze sliced toward the silent Andrew with an icy threat. "I saw you being forced into this carriage and I . . ."

With attention directed upon her brother, Hart did not notice the burly gentleman that slid behind him holding a large cudgel above his head. Not even when it came whizzing through the air and landed directly across the base of his neck.

"Caleb, no," shouted Andrew a second too late as Hart slumped forward to land at Molly's feet.

"Hart." With her heart lodged in her throat,

Molly slipped off her seat to kneel next to Hart's unconscious form. Then with tender care, she ran her fingers through his thick hair to discover the bump already swelling. Glancing up at her brother, she glared at him with a tide of fury. "My God, what have you done?"

There was a decided lump in the pit of Georgie's stomach as she restlessly paced the floor of her parlor. Well, perhaps not so much a lump, she decided. It was more like a heavy chunk of granite that was making her feel more than a bit ill.

Had she made a mistake in sending for Andrew?

It had seemed utterly necessary last evening when she had seen Molly so distraught.

As a woman who had suffered the pangs of a broken heart, she knew the signs of impending doom when she witnessed them.

The barely suppressed tears. The overwrought nerves. The desire to flee from the pain and hide herself from the world.

Whatever happened between Molly and Lord Woodhart had nothing to do with money or pride or even fear, and everything to do with wounded feelings.

Still, now that she had deceived Molly and set her off to Andrew's carriage that would whisk her away from London and Lord Woodhart, Georgie could not help but worry.

Molly was bound to be furious. She was so determined to save her brother that she had willingly blinded herself to the dangers that swirled about her. Dangers she could never have foreseen and was far too naive to protect herself from. And she would no doubt hold Georgie to blame for bringing an end to her ridiculous scheme.

Would Molly ever forgive her? Would she ever understand that Georgie had only wanted to do what was best for her?

The bothersome unease plagued Georgie throughout the long day, and foregoing the numerous invitations that might have tempted her to leave behind the vast, empty house, she continued her futile pacing as the hours passed.

How many hours she did not realize until the door was pressed open and for the first time she noted the thick shadows that filled the parlor. Expecting one of the maids come to light the candelabras, Georgie slowed her steps to a halt as her butler stepped into the room and offered a bow.

"My lady, forgive me for intruding but a Lord Thorpe is below and demanding to speak with you."

"Lord Thorpe?"

"Yes, my lady."

Georgie's brows snapped together in surprise. She, of course, was vaguely acquainted with the handsome, devilishly charming son of the Duke of Harmond. What female with red blood in her veins was not? Despite her preference for golden-haired rapscallions, not even she was utterly immune to his wicked beauty and more than once his flashing smile had made her heart give a small jolt.

But tonight it was his close relationship to Lord

Woodhart that made her heart give a small jolt, and not in a pleasant manner.

"Did he say what he desired?" she demanded of her disapproving servant.

"No, ma'am." Malroy offered a faint sniff. "Although I must say he appeared quite agitated."

Dear Lord, this was the last thing that she needed.

"Please tell him that I am indisposed."

"That is unfortunate, Lady Falker, because I do not intend to be brushed aside," a male voice drawled as Lord Thorpe thrust his way past the bristling butler and regarded her with an icy glare.

Instantly alarmed by the dark cloud of danger that swirled about the looming gentleman, Georgie took a hasty step backward.

"How dare you simply barge your way into my home?"

His smile could have frozen the Thames at the height of July. "Oh, I will dare a great deal as you will soon discover."

Was the man foxed? Or worse, unhinged?

"Malroy, call for the Watch," she commanded, never allowing her gaze to waver from the very large, very angry intruder.

Expecting at least some distress at the thought of being carted off by the authorities, Georgie was caught off guard when his smile merely widened.

"Please do."

"What?"

"I am quite certain that they will be very interested in the mysterious disappearance of Lord Woodhart."

Well, at least she now knew his trouble. He was indeed unhinged. Utterly and completely looby.

"Whatever are you talking about?"

"Do not play the innocent with me," he growled.

"I am not playing at anything." She planted her hands upon her hips. "I have not seen Lord Woodhart since the last evening. And I most certainly have no knowledge of his disappearance, mysterious or otherwise."

"That might be more convincing, my lady, if I did not know for a fact that Hart came here this morning."

"Here? That is absurd. Why would he come here?"

The dark eyes narrowed in obvious anger. "To investigate a carriage that was hiding in your mews. He never returned."

Georgie nearly stumbled to her knees, her mind whirling the unmistakable beginnings of panic.

How the devil would Lord Woodhart ever have known of the carriage? Not even her own servants had been aware of its presence. And worse, what had occurred when he had stumbled across Andrew?

"A . . . carriage? In my mews?"

The nobleman was not at all amused by her futile attempt to gain much-needed time to think.

"As you well know," he snapped, taking a deliberate step forward. "Tell me, was it a deliberate trap or did you merely take advantage of the fortuitous situation?"

She swallowed heavily. What could she say? She had no notion what might have occurred if Lord

Woodhart had indeed discovered Andrew in the mews.

Oh, Andrew would never harm the gentleman. At least not deliberately. He had never been violent whether rake or smuggler. But if there had been a tussle, or if Lord Woodhart had threatened Molly in some manner . . . well, who could say what mischief might have happened?

"You have taken leave of your senses," she at last attempted to bluster, just wanting to be rid of Lord Thorpe so that she could contact Andrew and discover the truth of what occurred in her mews. "Why would I desire to trap Lord Woodhart?"

The gentleman's features hardened with visible disdain. "Miss Conwell appears remarkably eager to become Viscountess Woodhart. I would put nothing beyond her, or you, in an effort to achieve such an ambitious goal. Including kidnapping."

Georgie stiffened in anger. She would endure many things. Slights, petty offenses, unwelcomed advances and ill-concealed jealousies. As a woman on her own in London such things were inevitable. But never would she endure an insult to her dear, beloved friend.

"That is quite enough, sir," she retorted in icy tones. "I will not endure your vile accusations. I want you to leave my home."

The dark brows arched in an impervious motion that clearly spoke of his ducal ancestry. "If I do walk out that door, Lady Falker, it will be to go to Carlton House. Hart is quite a favorite with the Prince and I assure you they will leave no stone unturned in an effort to discover his whereabouts." There was a strategic pause as he stabbed her with a fierce glare. "Beginning with that mysterious carriage."

Her breath caught in her throat. "Are you attempting to threaten me?"

"Absolutely," he retorted without apology. "Now, do you tell me what I wish to know or do I fetch the Prince?"

For a moment Georgie considered daring him to do his worse. After all, there was no means to prove that a stray carriage near a public alley had anything to do with her, or the disappearance of Lord Woodhart. But thankfully common sense came to her rescue.

How could she risk such an investigation?

Regardless whether Andrew was connected to Lord Woodhart's disappearance or not he was still living the life of a criminal.

Dear God, if it should become known that he was a smuggler, not even his powerful position could save him from ruin.

Or Molly.

Squaring her shoulders, Georgie sucked in a deep breath and glanced toward the servant who still hovered protectively in the background.

"Malroy, please close the door."

Chapter Twelve

He had died.

And worse, he had gone to hell just as so many had predicted he would.

What else could explain the infernal pain shooting through his head?

Certainly no amount of brandy or endless nights of dissipation had ever created such a dull throbbing. Not even after one particular night when he had foolishly allowed an acquaintance to lure him to a cheap gin house that had served the worse rotgut known to mankind.

Of course, there was something odd about this hell of his, he groggily acknowledged.

Not only did he seem to be lying upon a soft feather mattress, but the hand of an angel was gently stroking his forehead in a soothing motion. An angel that smelled of lavender.

Lavender?

He struggled to wade his way through the clinging darkness. There was only one angel who possessed the scent of lavender.

"Molly?" he muttered.

"Hart?" Warm, sweet breath brushed Hart's cheek. "Can you hear me?"

Wrenching open his heavy lids, Hart regarded the woman hovering above him. It was his beautiful angel, just as he had suspected. But there was something wrong.

He took a long dizzying moment to pinpoint the trouble.

Her eyes were not flashing with anger and her lips were not tight with displeasure.

Instead there was a soft vulnerability to her expression and a darkness to her eyes that spoke of concern.

Instinctively he attempted to lift himself upward to reassure her that all was well only to fall back onto the pillows with a rasping groan.

"Bloody hell."

The soft hand returned to his forehead as Molly shifted closer to his reclined form. "No, you must not move," she commanded.

Hart smiled wryly. Her warning was astonishingly unnecessary. He could not move if his life depended upon it.

And in truth he had lost all desire to. Not only did her sweet touch offer a soothing relief to the pain, but she had shifted upon the mattress until her hip pressed firmly into his thigh. A most tantalizing sensation he was not eager to come to an end.

Still, for all his pleasure in Molly's presence, he could not ignore the fact that he was lying in an unfamiliar room with an aching skull. He might be a blind fool when it came to this woman, but he was not an utter idiot.

"Where am I?" he demanded.

There was a brief pause before she reluctantly

met his searching gaze. "At a cottage just outside of London."

Hart frowned. Well. He had not expected that. "Was there an accident?"

"No." Her hand shifted to his cheek, threatening to undo his concentration completely. "You were hit over the head outside of Lady Falker's townhouse. Do you not recall?"

It was a struggle, but slowly the memories began to return. His valet's warnings of a strange carriage, his hurried flight to investigate the potential threat and his disbelieving horror when he had witnessed Molly being so roughly abducted.

Gads, his heart had refused to beat as he had rushed down the narrow alley. He had been terrified that the carriage would take off before he could reach Molly, which perhaps explained his shameful lack of caution when he had managed to wrench open the door and discovered that she was seemingly unharmed.

Blast it all. He had allowed himself to be taken from behind, now he could only pray that his stupidity hadn't landed both himself and Molly in some sort of danger.

"You were being kidnapped," he said.

Surprisingly, a hint of color touched Molly's countenance. "Not precisely."

His brows drew together. "I witnessed that man force you into the carriage."

"It was merely a misunderstanding."

Hart was not at all pleased. Molly's flustered air revealed that she was not the hapless victim he had presumed. Indeed, there was a horrid certainty growing in the pit of his stomach that she might very well be involved in whatever treachery was going on.

"A misunderstanding." Despite the pain Hart forced himself to scoot upward on the pillows, effectively dislodging her lingering touch. He feared he needed whatever remained of his rattled senses. "My dear, a misunderstanding is appearing for an appointment on Tuesday when it was set for Thursday. Or bringing a lady roses when she prefers daisies. It does not include attempting to murder lords of the realm."

She bit her bottom lip as her hands aimlessly toyed with a ribbon upon her muslin gown.

"You should not agitate yourself, Hart. Perhaps you should have a cup of tea or . . ."

"The only thing I desire is the truth," he interrupted sternly.

For a moment, she battled within herself before at last heaving a deep sigh. "I feared as much."

"Well?"

She rose to her feet, moving toward a shuttered window as if she was carefully considering her words.

"I suppose I shall have to begin at the beginning."

"That is, as a rule, the best place to begin," he retorted in dry tones.

"It is also the most difficult."

Studying her delicate profile, Hart noticed the pallor of her ivory skin and the tension in her slender form. Against his will a portion of his rising annoyance faded.

He was a fool, of course. But what gentleman in love was not a fool?

"It can be no worse than the insanity we have indulged in over the past few weeks," he murmured.

Turning her head she offered a shy, grateful smile at his teasing. "That is true enough. Still, I risk a great deal in revealing the truth."

A tingle inched down Hart's spine. Was this it? Was he at last to discover the reasons for Molly's obsession with his grandmother's fortune?

"It seems you shall have to trust me," he said in low tones.

"Yes." Her chin unconsciously lifted as she sucked in a deep breath. "You know of my brother?"

He gave an impatient shrug of his shoulders. "Of course."

"When my parents died a few years ago, Andrew was not at all prepared to take on his position. He was young and reckless and more concerned with the pleasures of London than field rotations."

"Much like any newly titled buck."

"Unlike most noblemen, however, Andrew was not blessed with endless wealth. Indeed, the estate was barely making a profit when my father died."

A glimmering of understanding began to tease at the edges of Hart's mind. Folding his arms over his chest, he regarded her with a somber expression.

"He fell in with the moneylenders," he hazarded.

Her eyes widened at his shrewd assumption. "Yes, but how did you know?"

If she thought that he would be shocked by such a confession then she was wide of the mark,

Hart acknowledged. He had been little more than a child himself when he had come into his title and if not for the stern, at times overbearing, guidance of his grandmother he might very well have tumbled into the same dire fate.

"Because Andrew is far from alone in his foolishness," he informed her. "It is said that the streets of Piccadilly are paved with aristocratic tears."

Stark pain rippled over her countenance as she wrapped her arms about her waist. "An apt description."

An echoing pain lanced though his susceptible heart. My God, she must have felt so helpless as she was forced to stand aside and watch her brother destroy their family.

"He lost everything?" he demanded gently.

"More than everything. Once he had depleted the sparse funds from the estate, he began borrowing heavily from the moneylenders. He did not come to his senses until they demanded repayment. By then it was far too late for any possibility of settling his debts."

Although her tone revealed very little, it did not take a great deal of imagination to realize just what this maiden had suffered over the past few years. The death of her parents, the ridiculous antics of her brother and the loss of the future owed to her.

Bloody hell, it was a miracle she had managed to survive.

"And so your noble brother fled and left you to fend for yourself?" he demanded in fierce tones. "He should be ashamed of himself."

"Oh no." She took a step back toward the bed, her expression troubled at his stark condemnation of her brother. "He only pretended to flee to the continent. After crossing the channel he doubled back and has been hiding in this cottage every since."

Hart was not at all impressed. What was the difference if he hid in France or England? He was still shirking his duties, the worthless cad.

"Why the pretense?"

"His life was being threatened. Andrew thought it best to keep his pursuers busy chasing shadows throughout Europe while he lay low here."

Hart gave a low grunt. "He must realize he cannot hide forever?"

"Actually he . . ." Her words trailed away.

"What?"

She licked her lips in a nervous gesture. "He has hopes of restoring his fortune."

Hart gave a startled glance about the barren cottage that had clearly seen more prosperous days.

"Here?"

"He only uses the cottage to conceal his whereabouts," she said in low, obviously embarrassed tones. "He spends most of his time nearer the coast."

Hart was momentarily confused. Not only by her words but by her obvious distress. It was as if she were more mortified by her brother's current state of poverty than by his reckless behavior that had caused his downfall.

Odd considering she had always maintained a courageous dignity even when forced to work for his grandmother as a companion.

Then at last his befuddled brain managed to

put together the less than subtle insinuations. A hidden cottage. The lies to cover her brother's whereabouts. Time along the coast.

"He is a smuggler," he said softly.

She flinched, whether from distress at her brother's profession or at the fear he might use this newfound evidence to harm her was impossible to say.

"Yes."

Hart frowned at the extent of Lord Canfield's foolishness. "He thinks to restore his fortune in such a manner?"

"He hopes to at least gather enough to pay off the most pressing of his creditors."

"A rather risky scheme."

"Too risky." Her head slowly lifted to reveal a vulnerability that instantly tugged at his heart. "You cannot imagine how many nights I lie awake certain that he has been shot in the dark, or hauled off to Newgate. It is unbearable."

The fierce concern for her brother was nearly tangible in the air and Hart stiffened as he regarded her brittle expression.

So that was it.

Molly was not obsessed with the money her brother had so recklessly tossed away, nor regaining her rightful role in society. As he had begun to suspect, she had no concern for herself at all.

Instead she was haunted by fears for her brother and clearly determined to go to any length to protect him. Even if it meant crossing wills with the Heartless Viscount.

Hart closed his eyes at the surge of conflicting emotions. Wonderment at her loyalty toward her brother. A sense of guilt at having judged her so wrong for so long. And an overriding fury toward the gentleman who had effectively ruined the future she so richly deserved.

"That is why you were so determined to get your hands upon thirty thousand pounds," he said in rasping tones. "To save your worthless brother."

"You are quite right, my lord," a deep, decidedly male voice retorted from the doorway. "As usual Molly was attempting to rescue me."

Startled by the unexpected intrusion Hart wrenched open his eyes to discover a tall, golden-haired gentleman walking toward the bed. It did not take much intelligence to guess that this was Lord Canfield. The resemblance to Molly was striking enough to have given away the relationship to the most casual of observers. And Hart was anything but casual. His dark eyes narrowed with a smoldering anger as he encountered the pale blue gaze.

"Ah, Lord Canfield, I presume," he drawled in deliberately insulting tones. "So at last you decide to stop hiding behind your sister's skirts."

With the atmosphere in the tiny chamber bristling with pure male aggression, Hart was not surprised when Molly stiffened as she flashed a wary glance toward her brother. He was, however, caught off guard by the intensity of his desire to leap from the bed and take a swing at the too handsome countenance.

Not because this man was responsible for the pain still throbbing in his head. Or even for his illegal activities that might have outraged some noblemen. But quite simply because he had dared to fail Molly so abominably. A notion that might have terrified him a fortnight ago, but now seemed perfectly reasonable.

As the uncomfortable silence stretched, Molly at last cleared her throat in a nervous manner.

"Andrew. You should not be here," she murmured.

Lord Canfield gave a lift of his golden brows as he turned toward his sister. "Actually, Molly, it is you who should not be here. I did request that you allow me to tend to our guest."

The faintest of flushes touched her cheeks at the gentle reprimand. "I just wished to assure myself he was not seriously harmed."

"Commendable, but now I really must insist that you leave this chamber. It is not at all fitting for a maiden to be alone with a gentleman."

"But I . . ."

"Molly," Andrew interrupted in stern tones.

"Perhaps, my sweet, it would be for the best," Hart determinedly headed off the sibling squabble. Despite an undeniable part of him that regretted even a moment without Molly near, a larger part of him desired a few moments alone with Lord Canfield. How else could he vent his utter disapproval of his brotherly care? "I have a few things that I would like to discuss with my host." He lifted a slender hand as she shot him a startled frown. "Do not fear, we are both relatively civilized gentlemen. We should be able to hold a conversation without too much bloodshed."

Much to his delight, she moved toward the bed and laid a soft hand against his forehead. "You must promise not to overexcite yourself. It cannot be good for you."

Ignoring the dangerous glare coming from the direction of the young Baron, Hart reached up to grasp her fingers and gently carried them to his lips.

"I promise," he husked softly.

Just for a moment their gazes met, and Hart felt his heart slam against his chest. Bloody hell. Never before had he believed in spiritual unions. Or the poetic joining of two hearts. But the force shimmering between the two of them was undeniable.

As if unnerved by the violent surge of emotions, Molly awkwardly stepped from the bed before turning to hurry from the room. Hart watched her retreat with an unwitting frown, barely resisting the urge to call her back.

Soon, he assured himself. Soon he and Miss Molly Conwell were going to finish their long overdue conversation. There would be no more games or charades. No more hiding. No more denials.

Just a stark confession of what had grown between them.

And then he intended to capture his elusive angel once and for all.

The sound of approaching footsteps abruptly jolted Hart from his brooding. Glancing upward, he realized that Lord Canfield had moved close to the bed to regard him with a cold, piercing scrutiny.

"Remarkable," the younger man announced, a shrewd intelligence glinting in the blue eyes that spoke of experiences beyond his years. "I believe that is the first occasion that Molly has ever done what was requested of her."

Sensing that the gentleman was more than a tad suspicious of Molly's presence in the chamber, Hart shifted into a more upright position. Lord Canfield, or at least his minion, had managed to knock him senseless once. He would not be caught off guard again.

"Molly does what is requested of her only when it pleases her," he muttered. "Regardless of who is doing the requesting, as I am sure you are aware."

Andrew gave a small dip of his head. "True enough, although never with such tender concern."

Hart battled the most absurd urge to blush before he was sternly gathering his composure about himself. He was not about to be discomforted as if he were a school lad enduring his first infatuation. Certainly not by the gentleman who had blithely thrown Molly into danger.

"I believe that I have you to thank for this delightful kidnapping?" He determinedly took the offensive.

If he were caught off guard by the abrupt charge the younger man hid it well. Indeed, his reaction was no more than a faint smile.

"An entirely unintentional kidnapping, I assure you. My groom is rather protective of me and has a tendency to strike at the slightest provocation."

Hart grimaced. "So I have noticed."

"It would not have occurred had you not attacked the carriage as if you were Wellington at Waterloo."

"I thought Molly was in danger," Hart growled, unwittingly revealing more than he intended.

On cue Andrew narrowed his gaze in a thoughtful manner. "It was my understanding that you have done everything possible to rid London of my sister's presence. Why would you be concerned if she were about to be conveniently disposed of?"

"I would not hesitate to rescue anyone, including my enemies, from the hands of ruffians," he defensively retorted. "As would any gentleman."

"So you do consider Molly an enemy?"

Hart frowned in irritation. "I think I am the one who should be asking the questions, Lord Canfield. You are in a rather precarious situation considering you have kidnapped a peer of the realm. Some might judge it a hanging offense."

Once again his jab flew wide as Andrew gave a small shrug. "I fear that you will not overly rattle me with such dire threats. My sins are so numerous that I have long since lost count of the reasons I should face the gallows."

"Sins such as abandoning your sister to survive without the assistance of money or family?" Hart demanded, not at all pleased by the nobleman's blithe manner.

Andrew winced as his eyes darkened with what seemed to be genuine pain. "The greatest of my sins, I confess. And one that I intend to correct."

Pleased that the gentleman possessed at least some regret for his atrocious behavior, Hart nevertheless was not about to be easily fobbed off.

"How?"

For a moment, he thought Andrew might refuse to answer his question, then with an audible sigh the younger gentleman turned to pace toward the window. Although the shadows of impending nightfall cloaked his expression, Hart could sense the tension that gripped the slender form.

"By doing what I should have done long ago," he at last confessed. "Confronting my troubles as a man rather than a spoiled lad. There will be no more hiding, no more running."

"No more smuggling?"

Andrew jerkily turned to regard him in startled surprise. "How . . .?" It took only a moment for realization that Molly had revealed his secret to hit. "Ah, of course. No. No more smuggling."

"What will you do?"

"I have a few acres attached to the estate that are not part of the entail and a handful of valuables that can be sold at auction," he revealed. "It is not nearly enough to cover my debts, but it should give me at least enough time to approach the banks and old friends of my father who might be willing to negotiate a loan to help me get the fields planted this season."

Hart had not expected such a logical scheme. Not from this gentleman.

"Why did you not do this when you first realized your folly?"

"Because I have always sought the easy path." Pacing back toward the bed, Andrew ran distracted fingers through the golden curls that so forcibly reminded Hart of his absent angel. "It was easier to pretend there was no solution than to accept the difficult choices that must be made. Unlike Molly I have never been ready to confront life as it is, rather than how I wished it to be."

"Molly had no choice."

"You need not remind me of how greatly I failed my sister," he retorted in bitter tones. "Or my tenants. Or the one woman I will ever love. It is all deeply etched upon my heart."

Although Hart sensed that Andrew was quite sincere in his regret as well as his determination to make matters right, he was not yet prepared to entirely forgive him for failing Molly.

Perhaps because of his own lingering guilt, he reluctantly acknowledged.

Neither of them could boast of their chivalrous, noble behavior.

"Very poetic," he muttered.

A wry smile eased Andrew's rigid expression. "Yes, well, I do have a point."

"And what is that?"

"Molly will no longer find it necessary to fret over my safety. Indeed, she shall be able to return to Oakgrove as she has so long desired."

If Andrew thought his words would offer comfort to Hart, he was sadly mistaken. The mere thought of Molly being buried in the country, hours away from London, and more importantly hours away from him, was enough to make him bristle in protest.

"So that she can become a penniless spinster?" he snapped.

Andrew met Hart's glittering glare with a lift of his brows. "What does it matter to you so long as she is away from London and no longer seeking your grandmother's fortune?"

"She deserves better."

"Ah, well. Who can say what the future holds?" The gentleman returned to his elegant, casually indifferent manner. "Molly is a beautiful, intelligent maiden. Once returned to her rightful place there should be no difficulty in finding her a husband. The local Squire has recently lost his wife, and then there is the new Vicar. Both have always quite admired my sister."

Hart nearly leaped from the mattress at the outrageous words. Molly married to another? Over his dead body, he assured his clenching heart. He had not found the woman destined to be Viscountess Woodhart to lose her to another.

But even as his hands clenched upon the coverlet, he noted the covert amusement glittering in the blue eyes. It was obvious that Lord Canfield had deliberately been baiting him.

With an effort Hart conjured an aloof smile. "It was my skull that was injured, Lord Canfield, not my wits. I know what you are attempting to do."

"Oh? And what is that?"

"To prod me into making a declaration for your sister. It would certainly solve all your troubles to possess a wealthy brother-in-law."

The amusement was abruptly banished as a stark determination hardened the handsome features.

"I would not accept a grout from you, my lord. Molly has sacrificed enough. When she weds it will only be to a gentleman who loves and respects her. As you say, she deserves no less."

Suitably chastised, Hart could only nod his head in slow agreement. "Yes."

Holding himself stiffly the offended lord gave a small bow. "When you are feeling well enough, my carriage will be at your disposal to return you to

London. Until then please be assured you will not be bothered."

With a sigh, Hart watched the bristling Andrew stride from the room. Well, he had managed to vent his annoyance. And to discover that Lord Canfield appeared determined to mend his ways.

Now he could only hope he hadn't so offended the young man that he would stand in the way of Hart's desire to win his sister's heart.

Chapter Thirteen

Pacing the cramped parlor, Molly fretted and fumed as the shadows grew ever darker. Why the blazes had she allowed Hart to convince her to leave? Although the two had managed to pretend a civility in her presence, she would have to be blind and deaf to have missed the crackle of male belligerence that filled the chamber.

Not surprising, of course. Hart had been attacked and undeniably kidnapped, while Andrew was determined to play the role of the possessive older brother. It was inevitable that the two would desire to cross swords.

But while she had long ago learned the futility of attempting to talk sense to a man when his pride was ruffled, she desperately wished she were standing between them. How else could she be certain that neither would do something foolish?

Back and forth she paced, pausing occasionally to glare at the narrow staircase and to strain for any sound that might drift from above.

What could possibly be taking Andrew so long? It could not take more than a moment to explain that this had all been a horrible mistake and to assure Hart that he would soon be returned to

London. Beyond that they could surely have little to discuss?

Her stomach was tied in knots and her head more than a little light-headed from lack of food when at last she heard the sound of footsteps descending. Rushing to the steps, she regarded her brother with a conflict of relief and annoyance.

"At last," she chided as Andrew swept past her and headed directly to a hidden cabinet to pour himself a large measure of brandy. "What on earth were you discussing?"

Sipping the fiery spirit, Andrew turned to lean against a crumbling wall. "That is a private matter between two gentlemen."

Her brows snapped together at his condescending tone. "Balderdash."

"Molly."

She folded her arms over her chest, not about to be treated as a simpleton. A matter between gentlemen . . . fah.

"I want to know what was said."

"Why?"

"Because I wish to be assured you did not upset Lord Woodhart," she retorted before she could fully consider her words.

Andrew cast her a searching glance over the rim of his glass. "Would it matter if I did?"

"Of course it would. It is entirely my doing that he was injured. I could not live with myself if he were to become seriously ill."

Polishing off his drink, Andrew set aside his empty glass. "I assure you that he has suffered no more than a mild bump upon the head. Nothing that he might not have received taking a tumble from his horse, or falling down after a night of carousing. He will recover soon enough."

Molly blinked at his offhand callousness. Good heavens, they had been party to a criminal assault upon a nobleman, followed by hauling the poor victim to this decrepit and decidedly damp cottage. Surely Andrew should reveal some regret, or even guilt for their behavior?

"You are remarkably indifferent, Andrew," she accused.

"And you are remarkably atwitter. Especially over a gentleman that you claimed to detest mere weeks ago," he countered in soft tones. "Could it be that your feelings have altered?"

Altered? They had undergone nothing short of an utter revelation.

Not that she was yet willing to confess as much. Not when she was still struggling with the truth of her emotional entanglement herself.

"He is . . . less detestable than I first presumed him to be," she cautiously confessed.

For some odd reason her words made Andrew's lips twitch with amusement. "Ah."

"What?"

"I am not a fool, Molly." Pushing himself from the wall, her brother stepped toward the center of the room. "'Tis obvious that you have developed an affection for Lord Woodhart."

Molly was unprepared by the sudden pain that ripped through her heart. Or the sense of loss that clutched at her stomach. Or even the bleakness of a future stretching forward without Hart being a part of it.

Whirling about she struggled to maintain her composure.

"What does it matter?" she muttered.

"I should think it would matter a great deal," Andrew retorted in tones of puzzlement.

"No. Lord Woodhart will soon be returning to London and I am determined to seek a new position far from the City."

"Actually, I believe I have a position in mind for you."

Molly turned about with a sudden frown. "Not with Cousin May?"

"Certainly not." Andrew thankfully set her fears at rest. "But I have a sense that Lord Woodhart will not be quite so willing to simply allow you to disappear from his life."

Although she was quite certain that her brother meant well, his words only deepened her pain. To dangle such impossible dreams beneath her nose could do nothing more than lead to ghastly disappointment.

"Nonsense. He will be delighted to see the back of me."

Andrew offered a wry chuckle. "Oh yes, that is no doubt the reason I was just raked over the coals for having ruined your life, and nearly called upon the field of honor when I suggested you might one day wed another."

Molly's breath faltered. "You discussed me?"

"Indeed." Andrew folded his arms over his chest. "I had expected a furious reprimand for having caused him injury and instead was treated to a litany of my failings toward you."

"He is no doubt delirious from his head injury," she muttered.

"Say what you will, the gentleman is not indifferent to you, Molly."

Molly lifted her hands to press them against her aching temples. How tempting it was. How glorious to believe it could all be so simple. Her and Hart together for eternity.

But if the past few years had taught her anything, it was that nothing could ever be simple.

"And what if he is not?" she said starkly, refusing to recall the tenderness of his touch or the strength of his arms when they encircled her. Such thoughts would only lead to madness. "He will still return to London to have his pick of the *ton* and I shall still be a penniless spinster with nothing to offer."

Andrew stiffened in outrage. "Do not say that."

"Why not? It is the truth."

"No, it is not," he gritted. "Penniless you may be, but you possess far more than any giggling debutante."

She forced a stiff smile to her lips. "If you say maturity, I shall box your ears."

"There is nothing shameful in maturity."

"Andrew," she warned.

His expression ruefully softened. "Be at ease, Molly. I was about to say that unlike too many maidens you are sensible, absurdly courageous and blessed with a generous heart. All the things a gentleman desires in a wife."

She rolled her eyes heavenward. Only a devoted brother could spout such foolishness.

"Fah. What a gentleman desires is beauty, a

spotless reputation and a large dowry. Precisely the things I shall never be able to offer."

Taking a step forward, Andrew gave a shake of his head. "For such an intelligent female you can be remarkably stupid."

"What is that supposed to mean?"

"It means that Lord Woodhart has had every proper, beautiful, wealthy debutante in London tossed at his feet and all know that he has never so much as given them a glance."

"That is because . . ." Molly broke off her words, realizing that she could not betray Hart's secret past. "Believe me there were reasons."

The golden brows lifted in curiosity. "Such as not discovering the woman of his heart until now?"

"Andrew," she said in sad tones.

About to respond her brother slowly stilled his head turning toward the door. "What was that?"

"I heard nothing."

Ignoring her assurances Andrew slipped toward the window, his smooth movements revealing his hard-earned skill no doubt learned during his months as a smuggler. For all his skill, however, he had barely managed to crack open the shutter when the door flew open and a large, obviously angry man charged directly toward him.

"Andrew," Molly cried, rushing toward the intruder even as he grabbed Andrew by the lapels of his jacket.

"Where is he?" the man demanded, giving Andrew a violent shake. "What have you done to my cousin?"

Determined to rescue her brother from the crazed attacker, Molly discovered her steps faltering as she belatedly recognized the raven hair and fiercely elegant countenance.

Lord Thorpe.

A Lord Thorpe who was clearly aware that Hart was in their care and not a bit pleased about it.

But how could he know? How could anyone know?

The answer to her dazed questions came hurtling through the door a moment later as Georgie rushed into the cabin and with a squeal of anger launched herself directly onto the back of Lord Thorpe.

Hart was standing before the mirror fussing with his cravat and ensuring his hair lay smoothly when he heard the noise from below. At first he ignored the vague sounds, ridiculously intent on ensuring he appeared his best before seeking out Molly. But when the decidedly feminine scream echoed through the air, he forgot everything but dashing out the door and down the steps.

The sight that greeted him might have been straight out of a French farce.

Molly stood alone in the center of the room, safe thank God, but near the window Lord Canfield was being held off the floor by a belligerent Lord Thorpe while Lady Falker beat upon his back with tiny fists.

Decidedly startled by the spectacle, Hart halted at the bottom of the stairs. In truth he was not certain whether to rush into the fray or simply laugh at the absurdity of it all.

"Thorpe, what the devil are you doing?" he

demanded in a voice loud enough to carry over the chaos.

The tableau briefly froze before every gaze in the room swung in his direction. Thorpe's eyes widened as he dumped his captive onto the floor.

"Hart. Thank God. Are you harmed?"

Hart grimaced with a hint of embarrassment. It was not pleasant to admit he had been taken off guard by a common ruffian. His highly paid fencing instructor, along with Gentleman Jackson would be heartily ashamed of him.

"Nothing beyond a thick skull and wounded pride," he admitted. "What are you doing here?"

Thorpe flashed him a jaundiced glare. "Obviously, I am attempting to rescue you."

"Ah, and are you succeeding?"

"Blister you, Hart," his cousin growled, turning about to grasp Lady Falker who continued to hit him wildly and shove her into Andrew's startled arms. "Here, do something with this vixen," he demanded, before moving forward to regard Hart with a frown. "Have you or have you not been kidnapped?"

Hart gave a lift of his hands. "I have been assured that it is all no more than a misunderstanding."

"Being held captive in this cottage is a misunderstanding?" Thorpe growled. "Either you have lost what little remained of your senses, or you are delirious."

Belatedly noting the haggard expression that spoke of his cousin's deep concern, Hart swiftly moved forward and placed his hand upon Thorpe's shoulder. "Forgive me for my levity. Why do we not step outside and I will attempt to explain?"

"You can explain this madness?"

Hart smiled ruefully as he steered his relative toward the still open door. "I did say I would attempt an explanation."

Molly watched Hart leave the cottage with a sense of doom.

Oh, she did not believe he would use the excuse to speak with his cousin to launch an escape. He must know she would never allow him to be held here against his will.

But while he might return long enough to take his leave, she was well aware that within moments he would be preparing to return to London. Preparing to leave her life forever.

Casting a glance toward Andrew who appeared remarkably satisfied to have Georgie in his arms as he softly comforted her, Molly slipped from the parlor and entered the small kitchen to put a kettle on to boil. Under normal circumstances she might have been very curious at the seeming accord between Georgie and Andrew. They had after all been at each other's throats for long enough. She would also have a few stern questions for her friend. Such as why Georgie had sent her to the stables just when Andrew was waiting to whisk her from London, and how she had known to bring Lord Thorpe to the cottage to discover Hart.

These were not normal circumstances, however, and while she might half-heartedly contemplate the strange events of the day, and the vast amount of meddling that had occurred, her thoughts refused to remain focused.

Instead her mind was filled with images of Hart. Hart as he had so lovingly tended to his grandmother. Hart risking his neck to rescue his frightened monkey. Hart brushing his fingers over her cheek as he gazed at her with smoldering desire.

Every moment in his company seemed engraved upon her heart. Even after she had sipped her tea and forced herself to eat a slice of cold ham, she continued to brood upon all that she was about to lose.

At last annoyed with her uncharacteristic bout of self-pity, she forced herself to rise and retrieve an old shawl hanging in the corner. Quietly, she let herself out of the cottage by the back door. She had been cooped up in the cottage for hours as she had fretted over Hart and a breath of fresh air seemed far preferable to continuing her futile brooding.

She had always been the sort to confront whatever troubles came her way, and to do so without wasting her emotions on regret. Now more than ever she needed that inner strength. There were too many decisions to be made for the future to dwell upon the past.

Barely aware of the icy breeze, she stepped upon the narrow path that led toward the nearby river. She was not, however, so lost in thought that she did not hear the sound of approaching footsteps.

Whirling about she recognized the tantalizing form of Hart a mere moment before he audaciously scooped her off her feet and continued down the path.

Molly's heart lodged in her throat, not only in surprise by Hart's strange behavior, but by the fierce pleasure that raced through her blood at the warm strength of his arms.

"Hart, whatever are you doing?" she forced herself to protest despite the deep knowledge she was precisely where she desired to be.

His wicked smile flashed in the silver shadows. "I should think that was obvious. You kidnapped me, now I am returning the favor."

"But your head," she fretted.

"Indeed. It is still quite tender so I must insist that you not struggle."

Despite her confusion of emotions, his words brought a militant glitter to her eyes. She had been independent far too long to be commanded by anyone.

"Insist?"

His low chuckle echoed through the silent night. "Perhaps a poor choice of words."

Her heart clenched at the sound of his laughter. It was yet one more thing she would miss.

"Hart, you really must put me down," she said in husky tones. "Andrew . . ."

"Your brother seems to be suitably occupied at the moment."

Something in his tone made her eyes widen. "Good heavens, he is not fighting with Lord Thorpe, is he?"

"Actually, my cousin is currently on his way back to London after warning me that he has utterly washed his hands of the lot of us," he said wryly. "And your brother is quite devotedly attempting to calm the ruffled nerves of Lady Falker. Which leaves the two of us blessedly unchaperoned for the moment."

Any chill she might have felt from the frosty air was banished as her blood heated with a forbidden excitement.

Unchaperoned. A romantic moon overhead. Masculine arms carrying her through the dark. Anything could happen.

Oh, she was wicked. Very, very wicked to hope that he would use their moments alone to steal a kiss.

"Where are you taking me?" she at last managed to demand.

"Just far enough from the cottage to ensure a measure of privacy."

"Why?"

His expression became somber as he met her searching gaze. "Because it is long past time that we put a halt to our foolish games and discuss what has occurred between us."

That was not at all the response she had been expecting and Molly stiffened in alarm.

No. She did not want to discuss their inevitable parting. Not when it was still so painful.

"I do not think that is at all wise, Hart," she muttered.

"Actually, I believe it might be the first wise thing either of us have done," he retorted sternly, halting next to a large oak tree and slowly setting her back on her feet. Resting his hands upon her shoulders, he regarded her with obvious determination. "Now, we are going to talk."

"You are very arrogant."

"Perhaps, but this cannot continue, Molly. You must know that."

"I . . . oh, blast." With a jerky motion, she pulled from his touch and turned her back to him. Maybe he was right. It might be best for both of them if they made a clean break of it. If nothing else he deserved an apology for the trouble she had caused him, intentional or otherwise. "Of course I know. I was a fool to ever begin this ridiculous charade."

"Molly . . ."

"No please, let me finish."

There was a moment before she heard him heave a faint sigh. "Very well."

Clenching her hands together, Molly sightlessly gazed toward the distant river. Even without glancing at Hart she could sense him standing behind her. It was in the goose bumps that feathered over her skin and the scent of male cologne that teased her nose.

Only with an effort did she keep herself from being distracted.

"There is no true excuse for my behavior," she at last began. "When I learned of your grandmother's will, I considered it a gift from heaven. I did not allow myself to question why she might have wished me to be a part of her inheritance, and certainly not why she would desire the two of us to wed. All that mattered was that I could rescue Andrew and return to my life at Oakgrove."

"Hardly surprising," he murmured.

"I also thrust you into the role of villain. I told myself you were arrogant and ruthless, and in dire need of a lesson in humility."

She could feel him stiffen at her blunt honesty. "Because I held you in such suspicion?"

"No, because it offered me the opportunity to ease my guilt. I could tell myself that stealing a fortune from you to save my brother from his own rash stupidity could surely not be so bad."

"You were desperate," he said softly, revealing that innate kindness she found so disconcerting.

She gave a shake of her head as she turned to meet his narrowed gaze. It was tempting to allow him to brush aside her guilt so easily, but in her heart she knew she had to offer full honesty. Now that she had begun, her conscience longed to be rid of its lingering shadows.

"No, I was as selfish as Andrew ever was. I wanted to grasp at the swiftest and easiest means of rescuing myself. Even if it meant sacrificing you to do so."

Surprisingly he did not appear shocked, or even disgusted by her stark confession. Instead his expression merely softened as he reached out to grasp her hands.

"And now?"

A lump threatened to form in her throat. "Now I realize it is not at all fair to punish you for Andrew's sins."

"Just as it was not fair of me to punish you for Victoria's sins. We have both made mistakes, Molly, but it is my hope we can put them behind us and begin again."

She frowned, not at all certain what he desired of her.

"For what purpose? You must return to London

and I must seek a new position. There is little chance we will ever meet again."

His grasp abruptly tightened upon her fingers as if he were caught off guard by her response.

"And is that what you desire?" he demanded in harsh tones. "Never to see me again?"

She flinched from the pain that raced through her. "It is simply destiny."

"Only if we allow it to be so." His gaze swept over her pale countenance, seeking some indication of her inner emotions. "Molly, you must know that I love you. And that I want to spend the rest of my life with you at my side."

A panic raced through her. Why was he saying such things to her? Even if it were true he must know that she could never become his Viscountess. Not when she could bring him nothing but shame.

"Please, no," she whispered. "It is impossible."

His brows snapped together with impatience. "Why? Do you not return my feelings?"

"Of course I do," she retorted, shocked that he could doubt for a moment the love that shimmered through her. "That is precisely why we cannot wed."

His low growl echoed through the air. "You are making no sense."

Molly squeezed his fingers, determined to make him understand. "It is precisely because I love you that I wish to see you wed to a woman who will bring you only pride. Not a penniless spinster whose brother is stained with scandal."

Oddly, her logical explanation only deepened his frown.

"You listen to me, Miss Conwell," he said sternly. "No one was a higher stickler than my grandmother and if she thought you proper to become Viscountess Woodhart, then nothing and no one would dare to gainsay her. Especially not me."

His reprimand forced her to waver. Dear heavens, she had never actually considered Lady Woodhart's opinion. It was certainly true her ladyship was a high stickler. Was it possible the older woman considered Molly a suitable bride for her grandson?

She gave a slow shake of her head. "I cannot imagine what she was thinking when she made that will."

A wry smile touched his lips. "I can tell you precisely. She noticed a grandson who was fascinated by her paid companion despite his most fierce determination to remain indifferent, and a young lady who was slowly sinking beneath the heavy burdens she carried. And of course, the cunning old dragon could not possibly have missed the violent sparks that we set off together."

A cautious, but undeniable hope began to bloom within her heart. "You believe she truly hoped we would wed?"

Slowly, he shifted to surround her in the warmth of his embrace, the midnight eyes glowing in the moonlight.

"Yes, I do, but to be honest with you it would not matter a farthing to me. Nothing matters beyond the fact that for too long I have allowed myself to merely endure the passing days. It was not until you entered my life that I awoke from my self-imposed prison and started to experience the world again. You have filled my heart with love, but more than that, you have given my life purpose. You would not be so cruel as to take that away from me, would you?"

Nearly overcome by his gentle plea, Molly impetuously tossed her arms about his neck and pressed herself to his hard form.

"Oh, Hart."

With a laugh of pure joy, he lowered his head to press his lips to her own, the magic flaring between them banishing the lingering doubts that had haunted her for days.

This could not be wrong, her heart whispered. She may not be capable of offering this glorious man wealth or a pristine reputation, but she could give him an undying love that was surely worth more than all the gold in England.

Pulling back he regarded her with a knowing smile. "Tell me that you love me."

She framed his beautiful face with shaky hands. "I love you. I adore you. And I cannot imagine a life without you in it."

"That is well since there is no means possible of being rid of me now," he warned in only half teasing tones.

A joyful smile lit her countenance. "Rather like the plague, eh?"

He laughed as she tossed his long ago words back into his teeth. "Precisely. Do you mind?"

Molly lifted herself onto her toes to offer a tender kiss. "I cannot conceive of a more glorious future."

Epilogue

Much to the chagrin of London society, the wedding of the elusive Heartless Viscount to Miss Molly Conwell was a private affair held in the small chapel at the Woodhart estate. Only a handful were invited to attend the ceremony and even fewer the wedding breakfast to toast the newly married couple.

Of course the papers were filled with speculation. Not only because the Viscount had so determinedly avoided the altar for so long, but it was rumored that the long absent Lord Canfield had returned from the continent to take his place at his ancestral home. With the other illustrious guests to include the dashing Lady Falker and the always desired Lord Thorpe there was bound to be more than a bit of curiosity, combined with downright chagrin among those aristocrats who feared they had been slighted from the social event of the year.

Hart along with his beautiful bride were indifferent to the flutter they created.

Indeed, most watching the couple would concede that the two were indifferent to anything beyond each other.

Remaining arm in arm throughout the long morning, they absently performed their parts and managed to endure the numerous toasts and well wishes before Hart was impatiently calling for his groom and whisking Molly away from the sweeping Queen Anne home to the seclusion of his carriage. A seclusion shared by a tiny monkey attired in wedding finery.

Once alone, he tucked her close to his side and stretched out his legs in sheer relief.

He had done it. Despite the inner demons he had been forced to battle, despite the charades and devious manipulations, despite his bride's own ridiculous fears, he had at last captured his elusive angel. The woman of his dreams.

They were well and truly wed now. And nothing could come between them.

Unwittingly, a smile of pleasure curved his lips as he breathed deeply of the lavender-scented air.

At his side Molly turned so that she could study his relaxed profile, perhaps sensing his inner contentment.

"You are appearing rather smug," she murmured.

His arm tightened about her shoulders. "Why should I not? I at last have the woman I love irrevocably bound to me, and best of all we are rid of all those pesky relatives who refused to allow me a moment alone with you."

He turned to catch a glimpse of the soft blush that stained her cheeks. "Yes, well, Andrew thought it best to avoid any hint of scandal considering our already strange courtship."

A no doubt wise decision, Hart grudgingly

conceded. Molly was already anxious enough at taking on the role of Viscountess Woodhart without risking gossip. Still, there had been more than one occasion he had longed to strangle the overly protective puppy when he had remained bristling in the background during Hart's visits.

"Thankfully we are now wed and he can turn his attentions to his own tangled future."

She grimaced, no doubt recalling her latest battle with Lord Canfield over his stubborn refusal to accept Hart's financial assistance.

"He can be utterly exasperating," she muttered, then a faint smile touched her lips. "At least he and Georgie seem to have mended their relationship. Indeed, I have high hopes that in time she will one day be my sister in truth."

Hart dropped a kiss atop her golden curls, as always amazed by her incredible optimism.

"It will not be easy, my sweet. Lady Falker is a shrewd woman who will not hastily rush into marriage unless she is certain your brother has truly changed his ways."

"I suppose you are right," she reluctantly agreed.

"Still, we both know that the most difficult paths lead to the greatest treasure."

"Mmm." She snuggled even closer causing a most heated reaction within Hart. "You have not yet revealed where we are going to enjoy our honeymoon."

The heat became more pronounced as Hart swallowed heavily. "Does it matter?"

She shifted her head to offer him a sweetly

enticing smile. "Not in the least. As long as we are together, I am satisfied."

Yes. Together. His heart seemed ready to burst with pure joy.

"In that case, I shall tell you that we are going to fulfill a fantasy that has plagued me to near insanity," he confessed in husky tones.

Her brows lifted. "What fantasy?"

"The two of us very much alone at our hunting lodge."

The blush deepened to a near crimson, but her eyes flashed with an undeniable promise of pleasure.

"Why, Hart."

"After that you can choose wherever you might wish to go," he promised. "Paris. Rome. Brussels."

Astonishingly, she managed to press herself even closer making Hart vibrantly aware of every soft, scented curve of her.

"Actually a few days at the hunting lodge sounds perfect."

He closed his eyes to battle the rising tide of passion. "A few days. Or weeks. Or months."

Both intent on the thickening atmosphere in the carriage, neither noticed when they turned off the main path and headed up a winding trail toward a brick building set in a copse of trees. Not at least until the groom brought the pair of restless horses to a halt.

With a blink Molly pulled away to peer out the window. "Why ever are we stopping here?"

With a shake of his head to clear his foggy brain, Hart sat up straight and reached into his jacket to remove an official slip of paper.

"You distracted me so that I nearly forgot our first mission," he ruefully admitted.

Not surprisingly she offered him a puzzled frown. He was uncertain why, but he had wished to keep his wedding present for his bride a secret. Now he could only hope that it wasn't a disappointment.

"And what mission might that be?" she demanded.

Almost sheepishly, he handed her the paper. "This."

She quickly scanned the writing, her brow remaining furrowed in confusion. "A bank draft for thirty thousand pounds? What are you planning to do with this?"

"We are delivering it to the Woodhart Charity for the Disadvantaged."

"Even though we fulfilled the terms of your grandmother's will?"

He shifted uncomfortably upon the leather seat. "Well, the money has already achieved its purpose in bringing us together. Now it seems only fair to offer it to those who are in true need."

There was a long, unnerving silence and then Molly's beautiful eyes filled with tears.

"You just proved me wrong," she managed to choke out.

Genuinely alarmed, Hart regarded his bride with a searching gaze. Good God, what had he done? He had been so certain she would be pleased with his offering.

"What is it?" he managed to rasp.

Without warning, she flung herself against his

chest, knocking the wind and all thoughts out of him.

"I thought when we stood at the altar and said our vows that I could not be happier," she said through the watery tears. "It seems that I shall have to become accustomed to tumbling deeper in love with you with every passing moment."

Light-headed with relief, Hart wrapped his arms about his bride, silently sending up a prayer of thanks to his clever grandmother who managed to bring about this miracle.

"An arduous duty, I fear," he murmured softly.

"No." She pressed her lips to his own. "A wondrous dream."

Hart returned the kiss with gentle contentment. "A dream complete with my very own angel."

Please turn the page for an exciting sneak peek of

Deborah Raleigh's

Regency-set historical romance

SOME LIKE IT WICKED

coming in September 2005!

Chapter One

From the diary of Miss Jane Middleton, April 21, 1814:

Dearest diary,

I have discovered since my arrival in London that attending a fashionable ball is rather like being a player in a theatre production.

To begin with everyone is expected to know their character and their precise stage directions.

Older gentlemen, who are notoriously hard of hearing, are placed well away from the orchestra so they may bellow at one another without disturbing the dancers.

Matrons and dowagers are situated in a prominent position so that they may comfortably dispose of the reputations of the various guests.

The young, dashing blades and debutantes blessed with natural grace and beauty are allowed their privileged place in center stage as they flirt and twirl about the dance floor.

And last, and perhaps least, the unfortunate wallflowers are gathered together in a discreet, shadowed corner, rather like a forgotten, ill-tended garden.

Woe be it to any player who does not meekly submit to their proper role . . .

Miss Jane Middleton was frankly miserable.

She hated London. She hated the thick, black air. The narrow, crowded streets. The endless noise. The arrogant, utterly shallow *ton.* And most of all, she hated the painful, torturous humiliation of what was politely termed "The Marriage Mart."

Who could have suspected that it would prove to be as delightful as having a tooth drawn?

Without a mother to warn her of the pitfalls, she had simply presumed that all maidens traveled to London and were introduced to a number of gentlemen anxious to discover a wife.

She possessed no great expectations.

She knew she was plain of feature and far too outspoken for a maiden. She was also three and twenty, well past the age of a proper debutante.

But she did possess a sizeable fortune as well as an unentitled estate in Surrey that would surely be a temptation. It seemed reasonable that she could discover a kindly disposed gentleman who would welcome such material possessions.

How could she have suspected that she would be so swiftly judged and found wanting? Or that because she was not a Diamond of the First Water she was expected to politely remain in the corner, ignored and forgotten by the various gentlemen?

Really, it was enough to make any woman screech in frustration.

And it did not help to have her obvious failure made the source of amusement by those maidens who had achieved social success.

Shifting uneasily upon the hard, uncomfortable seat, Jane stoically attempted to ignore the two pretty maidens who had halted next to the clutch of wallflowers that had been thrust into a darkened corner.

Over the past few weeks she had endured any number of snubs, insults and cruel taunts from Miss Fairfax and Miss Tully. They seemed to take particular delight in torturing those poor maidens already suffering beneath society's disdain. She had swiftly learned the only means of enduring their rude taunts was simply to pretend she did not notice them.

Almost on cue, the tiny blond-haired Miss Fairfax loosed a shrill giggle as she pointedly glanced toward Jane. "Really, Marianna, is it truly not pathetic? To just imagine an entire evening spent without one gentleman asking for a dance, or even bothering to make his bow in your direction. How utterly embarrassing it must be for them."

The taller, raven-haired Miss Tully wrinkled her nose as if she had caught whiff of some particularly nasty odor. "You would think they would eventually realize that they are unwelcome."

Jane clutched her fan until she feared it might snap. Inwardly, she allowed a delightful image to form of the two maidens being tumbled into a large, putrid midden heap.

Or perhaps roasting over a fire. Slowly.

"If only it were possible to ban them. It would be for their own good after all," Miss Fairfax twittered. "Surely they cannot enjoy an evening of being snubbed and ignored?"

"Perhaps they do not possess the wits to realize that they are so ill-favored they will never attract the notice of an eligible gentleman? After all, they are desperately persistent."

"True enough, although I fear that persistence will not be enough to lure a partner to this dismal corner."

Miss Tully gave an unpleasant laugh. "Well, perhaps pudding faced Simpson. Or poor, doddy Lord Hartstone. It is said he requested a potted plant to honor him with a waltz last week."

Miss Fairfax gave a dismissive sniff. "Not even he is so doddy as to desire a dance with that lot."

Jane bit the side of her lip until she drew blood. Oh yes, she definitely wanted them roasting over a slow, hot fire. With an apple stuck in their shrill mouths.

It was not that she often concerned herself with what others might say. After all, she had been flouting convention since her father had insisted she be trained to take over his numerous business concerns. But the scandalous disapproval had never struck a nerve. She had known deep within herself that she was perfectly capable of performing as well as any man.

This, however . . .

This disdain struck far too close to the truth, she grudgingly acknowledged. After several weeks she still had not attracted the attention of a respectable gentleman. Or any gentleman, for that matter. If the truth be told, they avoided her as if she carried the pox.

At the moment, it seemed more likely that she would sprout wings and fly as to find a husband.

"True enough," Miss Tully drawled, and then thankfully, a movement distracted her across the crowded dance floor. "Oh, oh. Look, 'tis Hellion."

With a nerve-wrenching squeal, Miss Fairfax was bouncing on her toes to catch sight of the current toast of London society; Mr. Caulfield, a devilishly handsome gentleman who managed to send every woman in London fluttering like a batch of witless butterflies.

"Are you certain?"

"I am hardly likely to confuse him with any other gentleman, am I?" Miss Tully demanded in tart tones.

"No," Miss Fairfax was forced to agree with a dramatic sigh. "What other gentleman could possibly be so elegant or so handsome?"

"Or so rakishly charming."

"How utterly delicious he is."

"A pity he never pays heed to debutantes. That is the sort of husband I desire."

The blonde slid her companion a sly glance. "My mother says that a clever maiden could capture his elusive attention. He is after all a man and as capable of tumbling into love as the next."

Predictably, Miss Tully frowned in a sour fashion. It did not appear that friendship could be allowed to interfere in the all-important hunt for a husband.

"I suppose that you believe you are clever enough to win his heart?" she scoffed.

"We shall see." Miss Fairfax gave a shrug before wrapping her arm through Miss Tully's. "Come, he will certainly never stray toward these wretched creatures. Let us stroll closer to him."

Together the two maidens set off in determined pursuit of Mr. Caulfield and Jane glared at their retreating backs.

Really, it was bad enough to endure being ignored, shoved aside and at times given the cut direct. But to be taunted by two maidens without a breath of sense between the two of them was beyond the pale.

She was in control of a vast fortune, she managed her own estate, and she had earned the respect of hardened businessmen who would have sworn that a female was incapable of caring for their own pin money.

It was unbearable that she should be judged less worthy than those twits simply because she did not possess a scrap of beauty.

In dire need of a moment's respite from the choking heat and ill-disguised glances of disdain from the vast crowd, Jane rose to her feet.

Gads, she would give up half her fortune for the opportunity to return to the quiet peace of Surrey.

"A few weeks in the country would surely not be so dreadful, Biddles. There is certain to be a few odd companions rattling about and, of course, there is always the pleasure of avoiding tedious balls such as this." The gentleman simply known as "Hellion" leaned against the wall in a corner of the crowded ballroom.

There were any number of rumors as to how he acquired the title.

Elderly gentlemen were convinced it came from

his aggravating habit of shocking society with his outrageous antics. In the past ten years, he had disrupted
a ball at Carlton House by bringing with him a monkey that had promptly stolen Lord Marton's wig and
sent poor old Lord Osburn into a fit of the vapors.
He had attired his mistress as a young blade and audaciously brought her to several gentlemen's clubs.
He had made an appearance in a particularly bawdy
play and only last year appeared at his uncle's wedding attired in the deepest mourning.

Elderly women were convinced the name came
from his habit of ignoring respectable debutantes and openly preferring the companionship
of seasoned courtesans and wicked widows.

Young ladies, of course, believed it was his devilish beauty. He was, in truth, indecently handsome.
Golden hair that shimmered like the softest satin
was carelessly brushed toward features carved by
the hand of an angel. His brow was wide and his
nose aquiline. If there was a hint of arrogance in
the high, prominent cheekbones and square cut
chin, no one had ever been heard to complain.
Even his form was magnificent in its chiseled perfection.

And his eyes . . .

Those black, wicked eyes.

The eyes of a rake, a rogue . . . a sinner.

It was little wonder maidens sighed in rapture
when he glanced in their direction. And young
gentlemen futilely attempted to ape his elegance.

Only Hellion knew the precise day he had
acquired the notorious title. It was a day that would
be forever branded upon his mind. And one that
he had no intention of revealing to anyone.

"My dear, Hellion, have you taken utter leave of your senses?" The small, sharp-featured gentleman drawled softly at his side. "You know how I detest the country. All that fresh air and mud. It cannot possibly be good for a gentleman's constitution. That is not even to mention the danger of all those filthy cows that are always lurking about. Who can say when they might decide to bolt and trample some innocent victim?" He gave a delicate shudder. "No, no. I fear that I cannot possibly leave London at the height of the Season."

Hellion lifted a restless shoulder. He had no more desire than his companion to flee town during the fashionable month of April. Still, what could he do? His countless creditors were becoming positively vulgar.

"As enchanting as I find London to be, I fear it might not be quite so lovely from behind the walls of Newgate."

Lord Horatio Bidwell, more affectionately known as Biddles lifted a brow. "Surely matters have not progressed to such a dismal state?"

Hellion grimaced. In truth, he had managed to land himself in a devilish coil. Certainly not the first occasion, but by far the most tedious.

"I assure you that I have found myself at *point non plus*," he confessed in low tones. "I have never made a habit of living within my income, which to be honest is hardly adequate for a fishmonger, certainly not a gentleman of fashion. My extravagances hardly mattered as long as I remained the heir apparent to the Earl of Falsdale. Creditors were delighted to court my favor and I was just as delighted to accept their generosity. But now . . ."

The flamboyantly attired Biddles lifted a dainty handkerchief to his nose. To all the world he appeared no more than another ridiculous fop that littered society. Only a select few were allowed to realize the shrewd, near brilliant wits behind the silly image.

"But now that the current earl has chosen to take a wife young enough to be his granddaughter, your role as heir apparent has become considerably less secure?"

Hellion struggled to maintain his air of casual nonchalance. Who would have thought his pompous prig of an uncle would choose to wed when he was near to sixty? Or that he would select a bride barely out of the schoolroom?

It would have been humorous to see the old windbag making a twit of himself over a mere child if it hadn't made Hellion's life a sudden grief.

"Quite odious of him, I must admit," he retorted in determinedly calm tones. "He could at least have possessed the decency to choose a bride who was not quite so obviously capable of producing the next heir. Since the wedding, I have been besieged by frantic bill collectors demanding payment."

"The old earl cannot be trusted to take care of such nasty business?"

Hellion stiffened in distaste. He would flee abroad before he crawled on his knees to his uncle. "No."

The pale eyes narrowed with swift comprehension. "I see. If your uncle cannot be depended upon, then you must turn your attention to other means of acquiring the necessary funds. Gambling, of course, is far too unpredictable, unless one happens to possess a talent for cheating. And I have discovered to my own dismay that the lottery is not at all a reliable means of holding off the vultures." There was a moment's pause. "Ah, but of course. There is one certain means of repairing the empty coffers."

"Indeed?" Hellion smiled wryly. "And how is that?"

"Why all you need do is to turn your attention to the numerous debutantes. There seems to be an endless gaggle of them and more than one will bring with them a sizable dowry. Some of them in fact possess an embarrassment of riches. You could be comfortably settled within a month if you wished."

Hellion glanced about the elegant guests with a shudder. To his shame, he had briefly considered the notion of marrying a fortune. It would certainly put an end to his current troubles and ensure his notorious appetite for the finer things in life would remain appeased.

But somehow the notion had made him shy away in unease. Since his parents' abrupt death he had never intimately shared his life with another. He had no siblings, no close relations beyond his odious uncle. And in truth, he did not desire such an intrusion. Not when he was perfectly satisfied with the undemanding, transitory relationships he enjoyed with his mistresses and friends.

The devil take it, he was not about to become responsible for another's happiness. Especially not a romantic, starry eyed maiden who would no doubt expect him to hand her his heart on a platter. It was unthinkable.

"I am not about to put myself on the block to go to the highest bidder," he denied in firm tones.

Biddles eyed him with a faint smile. "A charming description of the Marriage Mart."

"But accurate."

"It would solve a number of your troubles."

"And bring further troubles." His lips twisted as he took note of the various debutantes giggling and flirting about the room. "How should you like to be leg shackled to one of these goosewitted maidens for your entire life?"

"Egads, that is not humorous, Hellion. I must insist that you do not even jest about such a notion," Biddles retorted in horror.

"Precisely. Which means I shall have to discover another method of acquiring the funds that I need."

"Perhaps I can be of help."

The soft, decidedly female voice came from behind the large urn, and both Hellion and Biddles stiffened in shock as a small dab of a girl abruptly stepped into view.

Hellion glared at the woman in embarrassment. Good God, did she possess no manners? Did she not realize just how vulgar it was to hide in shadows and pry into a gentleman's secrets?

Not that he could entirely blame her for preferring the shadows, he unkindly concluded. She certainly possessed no beauty to put upon display. She was too slender and too dark for the current fashion with curls unbecomingly scraped from her gamine countenance and skin more olive than alabaster. Her only saving grace appeared to be her large blue eyes, although they met his gaze squarely rather than from beneath lowered lashes as was only proper.

"Who the devil are you?" he growled.

"Miss Middleton," she retorted, not seeming to be at all intimidated by his simmering anger. "Forgive me for intruding, but I could not help but overhear your conversation."

Hellion thinned his lips in displeasure. "Could not? How extraordinarily odd. Were you stuck to the floor? Or perhaps you forgot how to place one foot before the other so that you could politely move away?"

She at least possessed the grace to blush. Hellion noted the dark color did nothing to enhance her plain features.

"No, I was not stuck to the floor, nor did I forget how to walk," she surprised him by admitting. "In truth, I deliberately remained to listen."

Caught off guard by her honesty, he furrowed his brows. "Why?"

She seemed to hesitate as if debating within her own mind before slowly squaring her shoulders. "I believe that we may be of service to one another, Mr. Caulfield."

"Service?"

"I . . ." She glanced over her shoulder at the guests who even now were sending speculative glances in their direction. "I have a proposition for you."

Hellion stilled.

A pox on the chit.

Did she think she could use his secret to force him into marriage? She would not be the first maiden to use such despicable methods to try and acquire him as a husband.

"You are mistaken, Miss Middleton," he stated in a cold tone. "There is no proposition that a virgin could offer that would possibly interest me. I have no patience with debutantes or their tedious attentions."

"I am well aware of your preference for more sophisticated ladies," she retorted wryly. "Indeed, all of society is aware of your unfortunate . . . habits."

"Then what do you want?"

"The proposition I wish to offer you is one of a business nature."

Hellion did not believe her for a moment. What could this chit know of business? She must think him daft.

"Then once again I must disappoint you, Miss Middleton. My only business is pleasure," he drawled.

Something that might have been distaste rippled over the tiny countenance, but the features swiftly hardened with determination. "I am willing to offer you five thousand pounds."

Hellion gave a choked noise.

It was not often he was caught so completely off guard.

Five thousand pounds? It was a veritable fortune.

Certainly, it would put an end to his most pressing creditors. And most important of all, allow him to avoid the painful necessity of turning to his uncle for charity. But even as the dazzling thoughts were spinning through his mind, his common sense was whispering that such a fortune never came without a price.

He folded his arms over his chest as he regarded the maiden with a brooding intensity. "Very well, Miss Middleton, you have my attention."

She did not appear overwhelmed by his capitulation. Instead she once again glanced over her shoulder. "Perhaps it would be best if we conducted our conversation in a place that is less crowded."

Hellion hesitated.

To be alone with a maiden could spell certain disaster. One scream and he would find himself hauled down the altar before he could bolt.

Still, he could not deny he was intrigued. If she were seeking to trap him into marriage, she was at least the most original. And he had no doubt he was far too wily to be caught. No matter how clever the trap.

"Your notion has merit," he agreed with a rather mocking smile. "One can never be certain when there might be a sly eavesdropper lurking about the shadows."

The blush returned, but her pointed chin tilted to a determined angle. "Yes."

"Then shall we repair to the gardens?" he suggested, holding out his arm.

She hesitated only a moment before lightly placing her fingers upon his sleeve.

Hellion deliberately glanced toward Biddles who had all but disappeared into the shadows. With the slightest nod of his head, the flamboy-

ant dandy slipped through the crowd. He would
be waiting in the garden to avert any unpleasant
surprises.

In silence Hellion led his odd damsel toward the
open balcony. He did not doubt his choice in companions would be the fodder for the gossips on
the morrow. It did not trouble him unduly. He
had been upon the tongues of the rattles for years.

Once on the balcony he continued down the
curved staircase until they were at last in the relative privacy of the shadowed garden. Although
Hellion had seen no hint of Biddles he possessed
full faith he was nearby.

"Well, my dear." He drew to a halt turning to
regard her in the faint wash of moonlight. "This
is as private as we dare."

Her hand abruptly dropped from his arm and
he heard the sound of her rasping breath.

So, she was not nearly as confident and self-
assured as she liked to appear. The notion
pleased him. He far preferred to be the one
in command of any situation.

"Yes." Her hands briefly fluttered as if she
were not quite certain what to do with them before clasping them together at her waist. "I . . .
did you know we have been introduced before
this evening?"

Hellion lifted his brows in disbelief. Surely to
heaven she had not lured him out here to chas-
tise him for forgetting a previous introduction?
Hell's teeth, he was introduced to an endless
parade of debutantes every evening. Not even
he was rake enough to recall them all.

"Then it appears I owe you an apology, Miss

Middleton. My deepest regrets for my wretched memory."

Surprisingly, her lips twitched with a wry humor. "I did not reveal our previous encounter to badger for an apology, Mr. Caulfield. I simply wished to reveal my dilemma."

"Dilemma?"

"You are not the first gentleman to have forgotten an introduction to me," she confessed in low tones. "To be brutally frank no gentleman recalls my name. Or if they do, they attempt their best to pretend as if they do not."

His brows rose. "Surely you exaggerate?"

"Oh no, I am a practical woman, you see. I realize that I am old enough to be upon the shelf and that I have no claim to beauty. I suppose some might even consider me a fright. Even worse I have never developed the sort of silly charms that gentlemen seem to prefer. I do not giggle or flirt or pout. I am outspoken and prefer honesty to flirtation."

Hellion was arrested by her blunt honesty.

What other woman would so baldly claim her lack of charms? Especially to an unattached gentleman. She was either the most original maiden he had ever encountered, or she was unhinged.

His attention fully captured, he regarded the strange elfin face. For the first time he noted the full sweetness of her lips and the pure lines of her features. No, she would never be considered a beauty, but there was a measure of charm that would not be ravaged by time.

"I see."

"My hope was that my fortune would allow

potential suitors to overlook my numerous faults. Even if the money does smell of the shop."

He gave a choked sound of disbelief. "You desire to be wed for your fortune?"

She shrugged, her straightforward gaze never wavering. "As I said, I am practical. Can you foresee any gentleman tumbling into love with me?"

Hellion bit back the charming denial that rose to his lips. This Miss Middleton was not just another twittering debutante. She would never accept the shallow lies that formed the usual conversations in society.

She was not a beauty. She was not lushly formed. Still, she was clearly intelligent and eccentric enough not to be a bore.

And there was that startling sensual mouth . . .

A mouth that would no doubt bring endless pleasure to a gentleman with the patience to tutor her in the delights of passion.

"Who can say what the future might bring?" he at last hedged.

"I do not have the patience to await such an unlikely event." She abruptly stepped closer, her large eyes oddly luminescent in the moonlight. "I wish to be wed while I am still capable of producing children. That is why I requested to speak with you."

Unease prickled over his skin. There was an unmistakable expression of determination upon her countenance. She was a woman upon a mission. And at the moment, he was standing directly in her path.

His eyes slowly narrowed. "You have decided to buy a husband and your thoughts turned to me?"

"Yes."

The dangerous fury threatened to return.

Had she thought of purchasing him simply because she had overheard his impulsive confession of being on the dun? Or did she presume every male must be for sale?

"I suppose that I should be flattered, Miss Middleton," he retorted in dark tones. "But to be frank, I am not yet so desperate that I must put a price upon myself."

Her own brows drew together. "What?"

"I will not wed you, my dear. No matter what your fortune," he said in concise tones.

Without warning she gave a sudden laugh. Amazingly, the gamine features seemed to light with a rather enchanting mischievousness.

"Oh no. I do not want to wed you, Mr. Caulfield."

"No?"

"Certainly not," she said firmly. "What I have in mind is a kind, comfortable husband who will be content at my estate in Surrey. One that shares my interest in business and hopefully will be a friend as well as a companion. I have no desire for a . . ."

"A what?"

"A rake," she said baldly.

Well. That certainly put him nicely in his place. Hellion was not certain whether to be relieved or insulted. All he did know was that this bewildering creature increasingly intrigued him.

"It appears that I am being uncommonly dull-witted this evening, my dear. If you do not wish me as a husband, then why did you seek me out?"

"Because I am a wallflower."

He blinked. Gads. Perhaps she was unhinged.

"A wallflower?"

"It is the term used for those unfortunate maidens who cannot hope to tempt a gentleman into asking her to dance or even to strike up a conversation."

"I am familiar with the term," he said dryly.

She drew in a deep breath. "Yes, well, since my arrival in London I have been relegated to dark corners and placed next to elderly gentlemen at dinner. Such a position makes it impossible for me to encounter the gentlemen who might desire to wed me."

Although vaguely familiar with the clutch of maidens who routinely lurked in the shadows of whatever room they entered, Hellion never gave them much thought. Of course, he rarely gave any proper maiden much thought.

"Rather hard luck, but you will eventually discover a gentleman you desire."

"And how precisely am I to do that?" she demanded, her hands dropping so that they could ball in frustration at her sides. "There appears to be no more hideous fate than to be seen in the company of a wallflower. I am rather like the plague."

"The plague?"

"Avoided at all cost. I suppose they fear my unpopularity is contagious."

He choked on an unflattering laugh. "Surely you exaggerate?"

"I only wish that I did," she said in grim tones. "Thus far I have been approached by one rakehell who is so desperate for wealth he would wed the devil himself, and a gentleman old enough to be my grandfather. All other suitors pretend that I do not even exist."

Hellion studied the small, somber face. It was obvious her adventure to London had proven to be a terrible disappointment. And yet, she had not given into despair. There were no tears, no melancholy.

Only that unmistakable air of determination.

"And what service do you believe I can perform?"

"I wish you to strike up a flirtation with me."

"I beg your pardon?"

"It has not escaped my notice that you are the undoubted leader of society."

"An empty title I can readily assure you, my dear," he said dryly.

"Hardly empty," she argued, her tongue reaching out to wet her full bottom lip. The gesture revealed she was not utterly unaware of the unconventional nature of their conversation. And unexpectedly sent a tingle of sharp heat through his thighs. Damn. Why the devil was he suddenly imagining those lips pressing to his skin, teasing and skimming ever downward? It was startlingly erotic. "If you are seen to speak with a maiden or offer her a dance, she is swiftly surrounded by a bevy of gentlemen hoping to follow your lead."

Hellion abruptly cleared his throat. "I believe that you greatly overestimate my power."

"Not at all. Only last evening you were seen to take Miss Valstone to dinner and she was nearly mobbed when she returned to the dance floor."

Hellion was polite enough not to mention Miss Valstone was considerably prettier than poor Miss Middleton and a consummate flirt.

"Surely you do not believe that a flirtation with me will allow you to become the Toast of the Season?" he questioned gently.

She smiled in a knowing manner as if able to read the disbelief he attempted to disguise. "I am not a fool. I assure you my only hope is to leave the shadows long enough to discover a gentleman that I can respect enough to wed. My wealth must count as some inducement."

Somehow her calm assumption that her only charm was in her bank account brought a frown to Hellion's brow. "You would respect a gentleman who would wed you for your fortune?"

She lifted her hands in a dismissive manner. "Marriages based upon need rather than affection are not so uncommon. Indeed, my own mother came from an aristocratic family who had fallen upon difficult times. The marriage was proposed by my grandfather to restore their faltering estate even though my father was a merchant."

"Such marriages may not be uncommon, but I would hardly think it would be the desire of most maidens."

A reminiscent expression softened the tiny features and deepened the blue of her eyes. "Although it was not a love match, my parents did develop a deep friendship that was unwavering until their death. In truth, I believe their respect for one another was far more vital and enduring than any passing fancy could have been. And quite necessary considering . . ."

His frown deepened. "Considering what?"

A brief silence descended at his abrupt question as if she judged whether he was truly interested or simply being polite. At last she gave a faint shrug.

"You must know that being from such different social positions ensured that they were not accepted in either. My father was not welcome among the aristocracy, and my mother made those among the merchants uneasy. It was . . . awkward for us, to say the least. Still, they were happy together. And that is what I desire."

Hellion slowly stiffened. Her words echoed far too close to his past. The isolation. The loneliness. The fear that there would never be a place in the world where he could truly belong.

Then he abruptly realized that unlike him, this maiden had determined upon her path and was prepared to do whatever necessary to achieve her goal.

A wholly unexpected pang of envy struck deep within Hellion.

It was absurd.

This poor chit had been a spectacular failure in society. She, herself, admitted that she was a wall-flower. She was even forced into the ignoble position of purchasing her husband.

And yet . . .

And yet there was absolute courage in her bold scheme. She was not content to allow failure to steal her dream. Rather than scampering home in embarrassment, as most young maidens would have done, she simply had considered the matter and determined upon a daring path.

Could he claim such valor? Did he confront his

troubles in his life with such admirable spirit? The very fact that he shied from even pondering the disturbing questions made him shift in unease.

Unaccustomed to being anything but utterly assured in the company of a woman, Hellion briefly allowed his gaze to sweep over the tidy, rigidly formal garden. He lingered just a moment upon the marble fountain that shimmered in the moonlight before at last drawing in a deep breath.

Only then did he return his attention to her watchful gaze.

"Miss Middleton, while I respect your very logical approach to marriage, I fear I cannot be a partner in your scheme."

Her expression gave nothing away as she continued to regard him with that unwavering gaze. "May I inquire why not?"

He gave a lift of his shoulder. "I have always made it a strict policy never to dally with debutantes. They are a complication I do not desire. If I am suddenly seen to be paying court, then all of London will presume that I am chasing you for your fortune."

The blue eyes widened as if considering his position for the first time. "Yes, I suppose that is true. No one would be foolish enough to believe you consider me a desirable flirt."

A reluctant laugh was torn from Hellion. "You are very blunt."

A measure of amusement touched her dark countenance. "Yes, I suppose I am. Like you I prefer to avoid complications. Unfortunately, it is not a trait that is much admired in a female."

"No, I suppose it is not," he agreed, reluctantly accepting the ridiculous, unwelcome pang of sympathy for Miss Middleton. What would she do if he refused to help her? Return home? Or worse, approach another gentleman who might take unfair advantage of her obvious naivety? "You are quite set upon this scheme, Miss Middleton?" he abruptly demanded before he could halt the words.

Her features hardened before she gave a firm nod of her head. "I wish to wed this season, Mr. Caulfield. I do not believe I could endure another London season. In truth, I would rather face the gallows. If that means offering you five thousand pounds to make me noticeable to eligible gentlemen, then so be it."

His full lips twisted. "You have no assurance that my meager attention will provide you the opportunity that you seek."

That smile that seemed to glow from her very heart abruptly returned. "Any investment is a gamble. I am willing to take the risk."

"You are a unique woman, Miss Middleton," he said softly.

"Then you will accept my proposition?"

Hellion paused.

He should tell her no.

It was not that he truly feared being labeled a fortune hunter. It had merely been a convenient excuse. After all, there was little shame in choosing a wife that would bring wealth to a family. It was, in fact, expected of by many gentlemen, even if delicacy prevented mentioning such a boorish subject.

And heaven above knew he was in desperate need of the blunt. Still, he was far too cautious to take her words at face value.

A young debutante was always trouble.

Marriage trouble.

"I will consider it," he at last conceded.

"Thank you." She briefly laid her fingers upon his sleeve before offering a small curtsey. "I must return before I am missed."

With swift, rather inelegant motions she had turned to make her way back up the stairs to the balcony. Hellion's lips twitched as he watched her retreat. She moved like a stable boy, he acknowledged wryly. And yet . . .

For all her lack of grace and traditional beauty, there was something about her. A vibrancy of spirit. A purity of purpose. And a passion for life that an experienced gentleman knew would be echoed in the bedchamber.

Ah, yes. She would be no passive mouse to close her eyes and bear the touch of a man. She would be a willing recipient who would give as much as she would take.

"A most intriguing proposal." A voice drawled from behind him.

Turning about, Hellion regarded Biddles as he leaned negligently against the trellised arbor.

"You heard all?"

Biddles negligently removed a rose petal clinging to his shocking pink coat. "But of course."

"And your thoughts?"

"Five thousand pounds could provide a certain measure of comfort."

"As long as Miss Middleton is to be trusted."

The long, pointed nose twitched. "You have reason to believe that she is lying?"

Hellion briefly glanced up to watch Miss Middleton disappear into the ballroom.

"Not at all, but after having been hunted by desperate debutantes and marriage mad mamas for the past ten years, I have learned to err on the side of caution."

"Most wise," Biddles murmured, although there was a glimmer of amusement in the pale eyes.

"I would prefer to assure myself that Miss Middleton is precisely who she claims to be."

"Ah, and how do you propose to do that?"

Hellion folded his arms over his chest, a slow smile spreading across his face. "Oh, not me, my dear Biddles. You."

Biddles gave a vague blink. "Me?"

"If there is a secret to be discovered concerning Miss Middleton, you are precisely the man to ferret it out."

Biddles lifted his hand to press his fingers to his chest in mock surprise. "Why, Hellion, I am wounded. What could a fribble like me discover?"

Hellion gave a short laugh. This man was the most devious spy England had ever produced.

"I have no doubt that you could discover the size of her slipper to her favorite color within the hour. What I wish to know, however, is if her fortune is as large as she claims, if she has any scandals in her past, and if she has confided in her friends a desire to have me as her husband."

"You believe this to be a trap?"

Hellion grimaced.

The problem was he did not know what he did believe.

Miss Middleton fell into no recognizable mold.

She was bold, intelligent and clearly capable of taking command of her life. She also managed to strike a cord of sympathy within him that he was not at all certain he wished to acknowledge. It would be sheer folly not to take the proper precautions.

"It would not be the first trap I have encountered."

"Anything else?"

"Yes," Hellion retorted with sudden resolution. "I want a secret."

Biddles stilled, his nose twitching. "A secret?"

Hellion's smile twisted. "My friend, you should know me well enough by now to realize I never bet upon a hand without holding the winning card. I desire a means of controlling Miss Middleton should she prove to be untrustworthy."

Without warning, Biddles threw back his head to laugh with delight. "What a devious mind you possess, Hellion. It is no wonder I am so terribly fond of you."

About the Author

Debbie Raleigh lives with her family in Missouri. She is currently working on a regency-set historical romance, *Some Like It Wicked,* coming out in September 2005, as well as a novella for a vampire romance collection called *Highland Vampire* (coming in trade paperback in September 2005). Debbie loves to hear from readers and you may write to her c/o Zebra Books. Please include a self-addressed, stamped envelope if you wish a response.

BOOK YOUR PLACE ON OUR WEBSITE AND MAKE THE READING CONNECTION!

We've created a customized website just for our very special readers, where you can get the inside scoop on everything that's going on with Zebra, Pinnacle and Kensington books.

When you come online, you'll have the exciting opportunity to:

- View covers of upcoming books
- Read sample chapters
- Learn about our future publishing schedule (listed by publication month *and author*)
- Find out when your favorite authors will be visiting a city near you
- Search for and order backlist books from our online catalog
- Check out author bios and background information
- Send e-mail to your favorite authors
- Meet the Kensington staff online
- Join us in weekly chats with authors, readers and other guests
- Get writing guidelines
- AND MUCH MORE!

**Visit our website at
http://www.kensingtonbooks.com**